SECRETS of
TOPSEA

THE EXTREMELY
HIGH TIDE!

SECRETS of TOPSEA

THE EXTREMELY HIGH TIDE!

Kir Fox & M. Shelley Coats
Illustrated by Rachel Sanson

DISNEY • HYPERION

LOS ANGELES   NEW YORK

First Edition, January 2019
10 9 8 7 6 5 4 3 2 1
FAC-020093-18327
Printed in the United States of America

Text is set in 12.2 Bodoni LT Pro/Monotype
Designed by Maria Elias
Illustrations created with ink, then colored and shaded with Procreate and Photoshop.

Library of Congress Cataloging-in-Publication Data

Names: Fox, Kir, author. • Coats, M. Shelley, author. • Sanson, Rachel,
  illustrator.
Title: The extremely high tide! / Kir Fox & M. Shelley Coats ; illustrations
  by Rachel Sanson.
Description: First edition. • Los Angeles ; New York : Disney-Hyperion, 2019.
  • Series: Secrets of Topsea ; [2] • Summary: "When Talise discovers a
  mysterious message in a bottle, she is convinced the message is meant for
  her—and it's telling her to build a boat"— Provided by publisher.
Identifiers: LCCN 2018033907 • ISBN 9781368000291 (hardcover) •
  ISBN 9781368000819 (pbk.)
Subjects: • CYAC: Friendship—Fiction. • Boats and boating—Fiction. •
  Tides—Fiction. • Supernatural—Fiction. • Humorous stories.
Classification: LCC PZ7.1.F6914 Ext 2019 • DDC [Fic]—dc23
LC record available at https://lccn.loc.gov/2018033907

Reinforced binding

Visit www.DisneyBooks.com

SUSTAINABLE FORESTRY INITIATIVE   Certified Sourcing
www.sfiprogram.org
SFI-00993

THIS LABEL APPLIES TO TEXT STOCK

For the kids who speak their own language

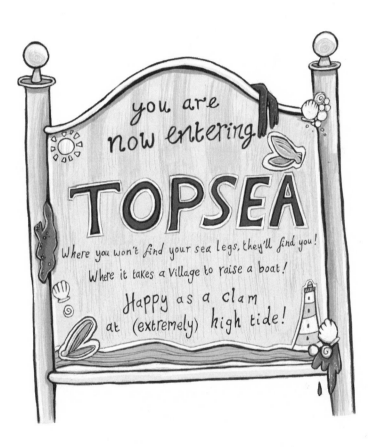

EVERYTHING ELSE YOU NEED TO KNOW ABOUT TOPSEA

by Fox & Coats

The Endless Pier

There is only one pier in the town of Topsea.

There are also quite a few docks. A boardwalk that would make a great racetrack, if you don't mind a troll shouting at you. But there is only one pier.

Fortunately, it's endless.

"Endless?" you might ask. "How can a pier be *endless*? Even the Endless Nachos at Nico's Taqueria end when he runs out of seaweed chips."

Good point. To figure it out, we should probably start at the beginning.

The beginning of the endless pier, we mean. It starts right here, on Topsea's beaches. Let's walk along it, shall we?

(Oops! Watch out for that broken plank!)

Everything has a beginning. And an ending, too. Like this book you're holding. There's a first page and a last page, right? Unless the rock cats got to it—they really like spoiling the endings of things.

If everything has an ending, that means this pier does, too.

But where? A little math might help. If the pier is twice as long as we've walked, that means we're halfway. Should we keep going? Or should we turn back?

(Look at those bubbles in the water. . . . Never mind, they're gone.)

How long *have* we been walking?

It feels like forever. But that can't be true. We know we started on Topsea's beaches, even if we can't see them from here. Before we saw the bubbles. Before the broken plank. We started at the beginning. Right?

Do we know for sure?

Maybe the pier *ends* on Topsea's beaches.

Maybe we started at the ending without realizing it.

And maybe, wherever the pier actually begins, somebody— or something—is walking toward us, too.

In the town of Topsea, there is only one pier.

Story 1:

SHLORPP!!!

S QUEAK!

"Drat," Talise muttered.

Quickly, she yanked her hand from her backpack and zipped it shut. She hoped nobody else in Ms. Grimalkin's fifth-grade class had heard the telltale sound.

"Was that a rubber duck?" Runa asked, leaning across the aisle. She had black hair cut into angles. Her cheeks had paint on them.

Talise was no good at lying. "Quite possibly," she said with a sigh.

"Rubber ducks are dangerous!" Jules exclaimed, leaning

across the other aisle. She had blond hair curled into spirals. Her cheeks had freckles on them.

"Not necessarily," Talise said. "They're only dangerous if they have eyes. I avoided looking inside my backpack just in case."

"Is anything the matter?" Ms. Grimalkin asked.

"Talise has a rubber duck in her backpack," Jules told their teacher.

Now everyone in class was staring. Talise started to feel upset on the inside. She disliked people staring at her. Possibly even more than rubber ducks.

And she *really* disliked rubber ducks!

Rubber ducks with rubbed-off eyes seemed to pop up everywhere Talise went. She found them stuffed in her bag of scuba gear. Hiding in her clam chowder. Bobbing in her extra-deep soaking bathtub. Once, she'd heard a knock at the door and opened it to find rubbed-off eyes gazing at her from the front porch.

Ms. Grimalkin walked over to Talise's desk. "Do you have a rubber duck in your backpack, Talise?" she asked.

"I may or may not." It wasn't a lie, because Talise hadn't actually *seen* the rubber duck.

"That doesn't make sense," Jules protested.

"Sure it does," Runa said helpfully. "If you think about it, *everybody's* backpacks may or may not have rubber ducks in them."

Quincy gasped so hard his glasses fell off. "Oh dear!"

Davy scratched his head. "Wait—both can't be true at the same time."

"Unless *neither* is!" Nia said dramatically.

4

"Nobody can be sure until they check," Finn added in a diplomatic manner.

Ms. Grimalkin massaged her temples. "That's enough, everyone. Talise, would you please unzip your backpack?"

Talise unzipped her backpack. A rubber duck stared back at her. It didn't have any eyes, but her classmates still recoiled.

"Drat," Talise said. She disliked rubber ducks staring at her most of all.

While the other kids went to recess, Talise joined Ms. Grimalkin at her desk. She had stripy-looking gray hair and extremely sharp nails. But behind her tortoiseshell glasses, her eyes were kind. "Why did you bring a rubber duck to school, Talise?" she asked.

"I thought it was my sea blob," Talise replied.

"Your *sea blob*?"

"Not a live sea blob, an inanimate one. Made of foam. Clara gave it to me." Clara was Talise's therapist. They met once a week and talked about all kinds of things. She had told Talise to squeeze the sea blob anytime she felt anxious. "I was very tired this morning. I must have grabbed a rubber duck instead."

"I'm glad your sessions with Clara have been helpful," Ms. Grimalkin said. "But why were you tired this morning?"

"Because of the ocean."

"The ocean?"

"I was working on my math homework," Talise explained. "Then I started thinking about how two-thirds of the earth's surface is ocean. And how ninety-five percent of the ocean is still undiscovered. You see, there's the deep sea, and the

5

deep-deep sea, and the even deeper sea than that—"

"Did you finish your math homework?" Ms. Grimalkin interrupted.

"I did not," Talise said.

"Well, thank you for being truthful."

"You're welcome."

Ms. Grimalkin drummed her pointy fingernails on her desk. "How about this. If you spend the rest of recess finishing your homework, I'll take the whole class to the beach this afternoon! What do you think?"

Talise nodded politely. "I feel very thrilled, thank you."

* * *

First, Talise pulled on her wet suit, flippers, and mask. Next, she strapped on her air tank, weight belt, and buoyancy vest. Last of all, she grabbed her depth gauge, underwater compass, and logbook: the waterproof notepad she used to log her dives.

She popped her regulator into her mouth. Then she flip-flipped over the sand to the rest of the class.

"Blurp blop bloop," she said.

"Talise," Ms. Grimalkin said. "We're only beachcombing today. If you'd needed diving equipment, I would have told you."

Talise glanced at her classmates, who were staring at her again. Even though the big blue ocean was *right there* beside them, they all wore land clothes. (Except for Nia's watch hog, Earl Grey. He didn't wear any clothes—unless you counted the teacup Nia had tied to his tail with a purple ribbon.)

"Blaaaaaargh," Talise sighed into her regulator.

There were many things Talise understood long before her classmates did. Like when Seaweed Season was approaching. (In approximately thirty-four days.)

Or what next Saturday's tide might be. (Severely Low with a threat of Wildcard.)

Or how to identify every tooth that washed up on Topsea's beaches. (Even before the Town Committee for Dental and Coastal Hygiene released its annual guide.)

As Topsea's only bathymetrist, Talise had studied the ocean more than anyone in Topsea. And now that she had a deep-sea-diving license, she didn't need to wait for a Vanishing Tide to explore it!

Her classmates found that very impressive.

But they understood many other things long before Talise did. Like when a wet suit was appropriate. (Talise would wear hers every day if she could.)

Or the difference between telling a story and lying.

Or each other. Talise's classmates understood each other immediately. But it took Talise a little extra effort.

"Sometimes, it's like they speak another language," Talise had complained to Clara during one therapy session. "Or lots of different ones."

"More like different dialects," Clara had suggested.

"What are dialects?"

"Dialects are different ways of speaking the same language," Clara had explained. "For example, Spanish is spoken differently in Mexico and Puerto Rico, where I'm from. Or Chile and Honduras.

Even in different parts of Spain! Once you've figured out your classmates' dialects, perhaps you'll understand them more easily."

Talise had liked that. "Do blue whales use different dialects in different parts of the ocean?"

Clara had smiled. "They probably do."

Once she had put on her land clothes, Talise rejoined the rest of the class. Ms. Grimalkin was handing out buckets and beachcombs.

"Collect anything odd or exceptional that you find," the teacher said. "According to the Town Committee for Tideland and Bath Toy Safety, even more peculiar items have been washing ashore lately."

"Oh, how *mysterious!*" Nia hopped up and down. So did her long, brown braid. Earl Grey tried to hop, but his hooves never left the ground.

"There is probably a logical explanation," Talise said.

"What's the fun in *that?*"

Nia's dialect was Ecstatic/Dramatic. One time, Talise's mother had arranged for Talise to play at Nia's house, and they'd spent the afternoon watching Mexican soap operas with Nia's nanny. All the characters were very dramatic. Talise understood Nia's dialect a bit more after that.

"Everybody, partner up!" Ms. Grimalkin said. "I'm off to find some lunch."

As usual, the best friends reached for their best friends. Finn reached for Runa's hand. Nia reached for Jules's hand. Davy reached for Quincy's hand. Talise reached for her sea blob, then remembered she'd left it at home.

Oh dear," Quincy said. "You don't have a partner *again?*"

Quincy's dialect was Considerate/Overwhelmed. He was probably the kindest kid Talise knew. He always thought about others—so much it occasionally made him anxious. That was a feeling Talise understood extremely well.

"I don't mind working alone," she told him. It was true. (Even if she had to remind herself sometimes.)

"She'll be fine," Nia said. "Talise knows more about the ocean than any kid in Topsea!"

"I know more about the ocean than any grown-up in Topsea, too," Talise said.

Jules raised her eyebrows. "Is that a fact?"

Jules's dialect was Clever/Overbearing. As the fifth grade's star reporter of the *Topsea Gazette*, she could get to the bottom of any mystery. Talise appreciated her attention to detail. Although sometimes Jules cared so much about being factual she clashed with her classmates.

"Because bathymetrists mainly study the bottom of the ocean, right?" Jules continued. "The lighthouse keeper probably knows more about the top—"

"Where is the lighthouse keeper, anyway?" Runa asked.

As the other kids turned to look at the lighthouse, Talise walked away. She glanced back once, but nobody seemed to notice she'd left.

"I don't mind working alone," she reminded herself.

It was better that way. Talise's classmates didn't really share her interests—and Ms. Grimalkin usually gave her extra credit, which she liked.

And as long as she had the ocean, she was never *truly* alone.

Talise walked along the shoreline. Currently, it was Low Tide verging on Severely Low, so there was a lot to see. Tide pools bustled with activity. Gulls and plovers pecked for meals. The air was approximately 67 degrees Fahrenheit, while the ocean was closer to 59 degrees. It would be even colder at the bottom, but that's what a wet suit was for.

"I bet I'd find tons of peculiar items on the ocean floor," Talise said.

But the assignment was beachcombing, not seacombing, so she began to search the sand. All she found was a flamingo tongue, a kitten's paw, and a handful of baby ears.

"Just a bunch of common shells," she sighed.

After a while, Davy and Quincy caught up with Talise. "Look what I found!" Davy said, his eyes bright. "Do you think it's a *fang*?"

Davy's dialect was Eager/Brave. He was the newest kid in Ms. Grimalkin's class. Everybody liked him, including Talise—even though he already seemed to understand Topsea's dialects better than she did.

"Indeed," Talise replied. "Do either of you have a toothbrush?"

"Why would I—" Davy began.

"Of course!" Quincy interrupted, pulling one from his pocket.

Talise used it to scrub dirt off the fang's nonpointy end. "I'm trying to determine if it has been broken off or snapped off," she explained.

Davy blink-blinked. "What's the difference?"

"Snapped-off fangs are mostly useless."

"Uh, I understand," Davy said. But his brow was furrowed, which usually meant a person didn't understand. So was he lying?

Talise was about to ask—but then she noticed an odd collection of bubbles at the water's edge, near Finn and Runa. She hurried over, then crouched down to check if any of them were rubber-duck eyes.

No eyes, only bubbles. Talise smiled.

When she stood up, Runa and Finn were smiling, too. "It's nice to see you in a good mood!" Finn exclaimed in his tiny voice.

"I am usually in a good mood," Talise said. "It just doesn't always show on the outside."

"Like the lighthouse keeper," Finn joked.

Finn's dialect was Friendly/Mouse. He was very polite, but also made funny jokes sometimes. At least, the other kids laughed. (When they managed to hear him.) Jokes weren't always logical, and sometimes it took Talise a little extra effort to figure out *why* they were funny.

"The lighthouse keeper does go outside the lighthouse!" Runa said. "One time, I saw her dive into the ocean and start swimming. She just kept swimming and swimming—even past the end of the endless pier. . . ."

Talise still hadn't figured out Runa's dialect.

That was because Talise rarely knew when she was telling the truth, and when she was making something up. Runa painted, too. Her paintings made even less sense than her stories. But then, Talise never really saw the point of art in the first place.

Sometimes, asking a question helped Talise figure out the truth. "Did the lighthouse keeper have the appropriate diving gear?" she asked.

Other times, it backfired. "Even I didn't believe that one!" Finn said, giggling. "The pier *has* no end."

Talise felt embarrassed on the inside. It made her want to jump into the ocean and keep swimming, just like the lighthouse keeper. Not just out to sea, but *into* sea. The deeper, the better. All the most interesting things were below the surface.

If Talise had the choice, she'd live in the ocean forever and ever.

She glanced away—and noticed the odd bubbles again. Even if none were rubber-duck eyes, she had a funny feeling about them.

Was there something interesting below the surface?

Talise flexed her fingers, then jammed her hand into the sand. At first, all she felt was a squishy, mucky sensation. It was quite pleasant. Then she touched something hard. She wiggled her fingers until they were wrapped around it. Using all her strength, she pulled it out.

SHLORPP!!!

The sound was so loud all her classmates came running.

"Is that a bottle?" Finn asked.

It was a bottle. More specifically, a barnacle-covered bottle with a salt-crusted cork jammed in one end. Talise pried it out— *POP.* Then she peered inside, keeping a safe distance from the mouth of the bottle, in case a crab tried to pinch her eyeball. It had happened before.

"Is there something inside?" Quincy asked.

There was something inside. Talise shook a small, rolled-up piece of paper into her hand. When she looked more closely, she saw it wasn't actually paper—it was a very thin piece of tree bark.

"Does it have writing on it?" Jules asked.

It had writing on it. All the kids leaned in to read except Nia, who jumped up and down exclaiming, "What does it *say*? What does it *say*?"

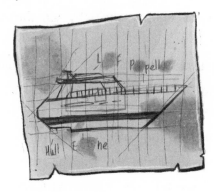

The kids all stared at each other.

"Hull . . ." Runa read. "Maybe they're just saying hullo?"

"Hullo?" Finn repeated.

"It's how they say hello in Great Britain."

"But look at the first letters," Quincy said, sounding worried. "They spell out HELP!"

Nia clapped her hands over her mouth. "Maybe somebody's stranded on a desert island! That happened in one of Nanny's telenovelas."

"You mean a *deserted* island," Jules said.

"That's what I said!"

"No, you said *'desert.'* 'Deserted' means there's nobody there. Is there even such a thing as a desert island?"

"Certainly," Talise said. "Some islands contain deserts. Of course, it depends on what hemisphere the island is located in, and also the size of the island. The larger the island, the more likely—"

"So somebody's stranded on some kind of island," Davy said. "Maybe."

"That bottle is *ancient!*" Jules said. "It's not trying to tell us anything at all."

At last, Ms. Grimalkin joined them. "What an interesting find!" she said, picking her teeth with a very fine fishbone. "Talise, I'm giving you ten points extra credit for your determination."

Talise kept staring at the note.

An extremely strong feeling rose in her chest. Like her very own personal tide. She didn't know if the message had come from a deserted island. Or a desert island. Or a deserted desert island. Or anybody at all.

But it *had* come from the ocean.

The ocean had sent Talise a message.

It took a little extra effort to translate, but she thought she understood. She didn't know whether it was logical, but for once, she didn't care.

"The ocean wants me to build a boat," Talise said.

Everybody stared at her like she spoke a different language.

TALISE'S LOGBOOK

Name: Talise Villepreux
Date: Friday
Location: Topsea beach
Time in: 2:00 **Time out:** 3:00 **Bottom Time:** None
Depth: Extremely Shallow
Temperature: Warm
Visibility: Slightly foggy

Observations:

My apologies, Logbook: beachcombing is not a form of diving. But today, I found it almost as exciting as a dive. I found a message in a bottle!

It appears to be a boat schematic, or a simple sketch that shows you how something is built. I have identified four words:

1. Hull
2. Engine
3. Luff
4. Propeller

The bottle is obviously quite old. There must be a reason the ocean decided to send it to shore *NOW*. I believe the ocean wants me to build a boat.

Do you think that is silly, Logbook? My classmates seem to. But they spend all their free time with their best friends. I spend all my free time with the ocean. Therefore, I am the kid most likely to translate the ocean's dialect. (With a little help from the library, of course.)

Building a boat alone will be a challenge. I suppose it's a good thing I'm used to working without a buddy. In fact, I would prefer to take on this endeavor alone.

Really.

NOTIFICATION: TEETH

Courtesy of the Town Committee for Dental and Coastal Hygiene

What's even better than beachcombing for seashells? *Beach-brushing* . . . for teeth!

Teeth are a very important part of your skeleton. They're also fun to collect. Here are some of the types of teeth you might find on Topsea's beaches.

Buckteeth: fun for parties

Sweet teeth: do not eat

Barnacles: these might look like teeth, but they are not actually teeth

Horns: also not teeth

Tusks: also not– wait, these are in fact teeth

Molars: for chewing

Elongated molars: longer than necessary, nobody knows why

Narwhal tusks: fancy sorts of teeth that are often mistaken for unicorn horns; one belongs to a magical animal, the other grows out of a horse's forehead

Saber teeth: these teeth are extinct

Snapped-off fangs: sharp, pointy, mean-spirited, mostly useless

Oolong: this is a type of tea, not teeth

Pincers: beware

Canines: whimsically named after mythological creatures

Beaks: not teeth—or are they?

Wisdom teeth: these teeth are quite valuable

Baleen: these teeth are a trap

There are many places to display your teeth collection: on your windowsill, under your bed, in a heavy-duty safe. Don't forget to floss!

Note: if you ever find a rubber duck with teeth . . . we don't know what to tell you.

THE TOPSEA SCHOOL GAZETTE

WORD OF THE DAY

Legible (adj.): ~~████████████████████~~

REMINDER

This Friday is Spirit Day! Students should wear comfortable clothes and shoes if they are planning to take part in "spirited" activities.

MISSING LIGHTHOUSE KEEPER!

by Jules, Fifth-Grade Star Reporter

It seems the tide isn't the only thing vanishing lately. Many students have expressed concern about the empty room at the top of the lighthouse.

Lighthouses are designed to offer navigational aid to ships, boats, and other visitors coming in from the sea. But without a keeper to flash the lights and sound the warnings, Topsea's lighthouse isn't keeping anyone safe.

This reporter believes the clues to solving the mystery lie in the lighthouse itself. Unfortunately, her parents caught her scaling the lighthouse wall before she made it to the top. But never fear, *Gazette* readers—this reporter may have lost her grappling-hook privileges, but she'll find another way to crack this story like a clam's shell!

Story 2:

Davy, Spirit Day

Topsea School had been buzzing about Spirit Day for weeks. After all, the spirits only visited once in a blue moon.

Mr. Zapple, the guidance counselor, hung banners in the halls.

SPIRIT DAY IS FRIDAY

Get Ready to Raise Your Spirits (Before They Raise You!)

Ricky and Micky and Nicky, the cafeteria workers, were planning a delicious soul food menu. And rumor had it Principal King got so carried away planning spirit activities, she'd accidentally floated through the wall of the kindergarten classroom and given them all a good fright.

Everyone was excited about Spirit Day. Except Davy.

All his friends had met their spirits back in kindergarten. But unlike them, Davy hadn't grown up in Topsea. What if his spirit didn't show up for Spirit Day?

What if he didn't even *have* a spirit?

"Should I look in the graveyard?" he asked Quincy on Monday at recess. They sat on the jungle gym, sharing Quincy's homemade chokeberry muffins.

"The graveyard?" Quincy seemed confused. "No, Ghost Day isn't for months."

"Aren't ghosts and spirits the same thing?"

Quincy laughed. "Of course not! Ghosts are okay at hide-and-seek, but they hate capture the flag. Spirits are really good at *all* games."

"Oh."

"Besides, you don't have to look for your spirit. Your spirit will find you."

Davy wasn't so sure.

On Wednesday, he felt more nervous than ever. "Are there spirits in the beach forest?" he asked Finn and Runa. "I heard there's all kinds of weird stuff in there."

"Nah, those are just made-up stories," Finn replied. "Well . . . I think they're made-up. Right, Runa?"

"Some of them are real!" Runa said. "But don't worry, Davy. If your spirit doesn't come to Spirit Day for some reason, you can share mine."

Davy's stomach did a backflip, and then a front flip. "Thanks, but I'm sure mine will show up," he said quickly.

On Friday morning, Davy stood nervously in the classroom doorway. His friends seemed to be chatting with their spirits. Davy couldn't actually *see* the spirits, of course. But every kid had an extra chair next to his or her desk. Even Earl Grey was snorting companionably with the cushion next to his.

Davy had an extra chair, too. But he didn't *have* a spirit!

He felt awkward and embarrassed. Just like his first day at Topsea School, when he'd walked into the classroom soaking wet.

Then he realized something.

If he couldn't see his friends' spirits . . . *they couldn't see his.*

"Good morning, Ms. Grimalkin!" Davy announced, stepping inside. He gestured to the empty air on his right. "I brought my spirit, as you can see."

Ms. Grimalkin squinted through her tortoiseshell glasses. Davy fidgeted. Could she see right through his lie?

Then she smiled widely, showing all of her teeth. "Hello there!" she said to the nothing next to him. "So glad you could join us for Spirit Day."

Relieved, Davy headed to his desk. He made a big show of scooting an extra chair next to his, then patting it for his spirit to sit down. Ms. Grimalkin took roll, and each student raised a hand at their name. Each spirit raised a hand, too. Or at least, Davy thought they did.

When Ms. Grimalkin called Davy's name, he raised his hand. She kept waiting. "Um . . ." Davy elbowed the air. "Raise your hand, silly!"

She added two checks in her roll book. "Your spirit seems a little shy, Davy."

"Mine isn't," Nia declared. "That's why we always win *all* the Spirit Day games!"

Talise looked up from the book she'd been reading. "Not *all* of them," she said. "As I recall, last year you and Jules tied in capture the flag."

"That's right," Jules said. "Nia's spirit tackled me right before I reached her flag, but then she tripped over a seaweed rope and—"

"Jules!" Nia exclaimed, looking mortally wounded. "You know that was just a fluke. This year, me and my spirit are winning *everything*."

Nia wasn't just the most dramatic kid at Topsea School. She was also the most competitive. Her biggest rival was usually Jules, her best friend.

But Davy had been the most competitive kid at his old school. He missed a good challenge! Of course, he didn't actually *have* a spirit—but so what? He'd fooled Ms. Grimalkin and all his classmates. Maybe he could be the first kid at Topsea School to win Spirit Day with no spirit at all!

Davy turned around in his desk to face Nia.

"Last year, I wasn't here," he said, grinning. "So winning everything might be a lot harder."

"Oh yeah?" Nia grinned back. "You think you and your spirit can beat me and *my* spirit?"

Davy pretended to give his spirit an appraising look. "Yup."

"There are three events. Best two out of three wins?"

"Unless I win all three."

Nia rolled her eyes. "Yeah, right."

They shook hands firmly. Their spirits did, too. Or at least, Davy hoped it looked like they did.

The kids chatted excitedly as Ms. Grimalkin led the fifth-grade class to the boardwalk. Talise trailed behind, reading her book as she walked.

"Is that about boats?" Davy asked.

"Indeed." Talise showed him the cover: *The Great Book of Boatbuilding*. "As a bathymetrist, I've always been more interested in what's *in* the ocean than what's floating on top of it. But boats are really quite fascinating."

Jules turned around. "You're not really considering building a boat, are you? Because that bottle was *ancient*! Even if someone did want to build a boat, it was a long, long time ago."

Davy noticed Talise's cheeks were slightly pink. "I think it'd be cool to have a boat," he said. "Think of all the places you could explore."

"But why build one from scratch?" Jules said. "There are plenty of boats in Topsea Harbor."

Talise frowned and went back to her book.

All the classes had gathered on the boardwalk, along with all the staff. Mr. Zapple, the school counselor, waved at Davy from where he stood next to Nurse Xavier and Cosmo, the janitor. Davy waved back.

Principal King wore a T-shirt that said *I've Got Spirit, How 'Bout You?* and was waving a huge white flag that read *Welcome, Spirits!* "Welcome, spirits!" she exclaimed. "And welcome, students. Are you ready for some Spirit Day fun?"

Davy cheered along with his classmates. Principal King cheered the loudest of all.

Once she'd finally stopped hooting, she divided the kids and assigned a staff member to each group. She sent Mr. Zapple off with the last group of kindergartners, then smiled at Davy, Quincy, Nia, Jules, Finn, Runa, and Talise.

"Looks like I saved the best group for myself!" She handed each student an extra-strong piece of seaweed. "Our first activity is the three-legged race. Make sure to tie them nice and tight—we don't want your spirits slipping free."

Davy tied one end of the seaweed around his left ankle. Then, glancing around, he pretended to tie the other end to his spirit's ankle. It dragged on the ground as he joined Nia at the starting line.

"Your spirit's looking a little laggy," she said smugly. Her seaweed swayed at her side, as if her spirit was jogging in place as a warm-up.

"He's saving his energy," Davy replied.

He twitched his leg, hoping it looked like his spirit was tugging at the seaweed. To his surprise, the seaweed actually floated in the air for a few seconds, wriggling. Then it drooped back to the ground.

"On the count of three!" Principal King held up her flag. "Ten! Two hundred! Five zillion and one! Seventeen-point-six! *Three!*"

She swiped down her flag.

Davy took off like a shot. So did Nia. They raced ahead of the others, thundering over the boardwalk. Nia's seaweed stretched ahead, as if reaching for the finish line. Davy's seaweed dragged behind him.

"Your spirit's slowing you down!" Nia taunted.

Suddenly a head popped up from a gap between two planks. It belonged to Billy, the cranky old woman who lived underneath.

"Why are you kids tramping all over my roof— *Egad!*" Billy shouted, ducking as Davy leaped over her.

Nia let out a triumphant laugh as she crossed the finish line first. She high-fived her spirit, then waited as Davy stumbled to a stop.

"That's one for me!" she said.

Davy rubbed at the stitch in his side. "Hey, I had a troll's head to hurdle," he protested, although he knew Billy wasn't a troll. He also knew that wasn't really why he'd lost. Nia was fast, and her spirit was even faster.

Davy was fast, too, but he didn't have a spirit.

All he had was a useless piece of seaweed tied to his ankle.

The next event of Spirit Day was hide-and-seek at the abandoned arcade. When Davy had first moved to Topsea, his friends had showed him how to sneak in. They'd had fun, although he was in no hurry to play Skee-Ball again anytime soon.

Today, the front doors were open. "Glad we don't have to crawl through the vent this time," Davy said.

Jules elbowed him in the side and put a finger to her lips.

"I forgot how much I love this arcade," Principal King said, gazing fondly at the moldy walls and sandy tile floors. "Why was it ever boarded up?"

Talise glanced up from *The Great Book of Boatbuilding*. "The PTA president said rides and games are unsafe," she said.

"Oh, right. Well, there's nothing unsafe about hide-and-seek!"

Scritch-scratch. A light sandpaper-scratchy sound came from behind the prize booth's rusty gate. All the kids took a step back.

"Well, there's nothing unsafe as long as you don't hide in the prize booth," Principal King conceded. "Okay, I'll give you and your spirits one minute to find a hiding place. If I find you, you turn into a seeker. Last student or spirit to be found is the winner. On your mark . . . get set . . . *hide!*"

She covered her eyes. The kids scattered.

Davy crawled under the Cave Escape pinball machine. He hoped the ghost who haunted it wouldn't mind. Luckily, the machine's lights and switches stayed dark, and the spinners and rollovers kept still. Quincy *had* said ghosts were pretty good at hide-and-seek, Davy remembered.

His hiding place machine made a great vantage point. He peered out as Principal King started seeking.

She found Jules first, because her curly blond hair was sticking up out of the fifty-point Skee-Ball hole. Then Jules found Finn curled up with the toys inside the claw crane. Then Finn found Runa behind the photo booth. Then Runa found Quincy crouched among the Whack-a-Moles.

"Ugh, we haven't found *any* spirits yet," Jules said, standing on tiptoe to check the top of the photo booth. "They're such good hiders."

"Being invisible is an advantage," Quincy agreed.

"Usually," Finn added.

Davy watched as the kids split up and searched. Runa found Finn's spirit inside a dusty glass cabinet filled with plastic jewelry—but it turned out her own spirit had been keeping his company.

"Shoot." Runa sighed. "Sorry, Finn. I guess we're both out."

"That's okay!" Finn said. "Our spirits must be best friends, too."

"Aha!" Quincy shouted from across the arcade.

SQUEAK! SQUEAK! SQUEAK!

Quincy pulled Talise from a display case—along with dozens of rubber ducks. "Oh dear!" he said, covering his face.

"Don't worry," Talise said. "They all have rubbed-off eyes."

"Whew." Quincy lowered his hands. "Good hiding spot! The rubber ducks really hid you well."

"Thank you. Although they weren't in there when I climbed into the case."

"Why do they follow you everywhere, anyway?"

"I wish I knew. It's really quite irritating." She shook *The Great Book of Boatbuilding*. A rubber duck fell out. "Oh, I think I see Earl Grey."

Talise hurried across the arcade, where Earl Grey and his spirit were hiding in the cobweb-filled vent the kids had used to sneak in. Soon the only hiders left were Davy, Nia, and their spirits.

Except Davy didn't really have a spirit. But no one else knew that.

Davy held his breath as a pair of tennis shoes came closer and closer to the pinball machine. Then Quincy's grinning face appeared upside down.

"Found you!"

"Aw," Davy said. He crawled out, then stared hard around the arcade. Where could Nia be? All the best hiding spots had been taken. . . .

Except the fortune-telling machine.

The *extraordinarily creepy* fortune-telling machine.

Bracing himself, Davy marched toward it. He looked behind the machine, then under it. No Nia. He looked at the Madam Flea mannequin inside. Wait a second—the last time Davy had

seen this mannequin, it didn't have any eyes. But now two brown eyes twinkled back at him.

"Found you!" Davy said triumphantly.

Nia pulled off Madam Flea's black wig. "You've got to admit, it was a good hiding spot."

"It was," Davy agreed.

Principal King cleared her throat. "If I'm not mistaken," she said, "we have two spirits left to find!"

Davy and Nia looked at each other. Then they took off running in opposite directions. Quincy and Runa helped Davy look for Nia's spirit. Finn and Jules helped Nia look for Davy's spirit. Earl Grey chased his spirit's tail. They searched high and low, and then Talise said:

"Oh, I found one!"

Everyone hurried over to the water spray game, where Talise was holding a water gun.

"I was reading about how tugboats perform a ceremonial water salute by spraying water, and I thought this toy gun might be useful for my boat," she explained. "At first, I thought it was clogged. But upon further inspection, a spirit seems to be hiding inside."

"Huh," Jules said. "At least all that boat research was good for *something*."

"How can you tell whose spirit is whose?" Davy blurted out. "They're all invisible."

Runa looked surprised. "Sure, but you can still tell. Look at Finn's!"

Davy looked at the air next to Finn. Was it a little bit Finn-shaped, or was that just his imagination?

Talise squeezed the trigger.

WHOOOSH!

Davy crossed his fingers behind his back. What if everyone thought it was his spirit? After all, he couldn't prove it wasn't.

But then Nia sighed loudly. "That's my spirit, all right. Guess you win this event, Davy!"

Davy beamed and uncrossed his fingers.

"Where *is* your spirit, anyway?" Principal King asked him. "We've looked everywhere!"

Davy recrossed his fingers. "Umm . . ."

Frantically, he looked around for a hiding spot no one had

checked. The sandpaper-scratchy sound came from behind the rusty gate again.

Nia clapped a hand to her mouth. "Is your spirit hiding in the *prize booth*?"

"Um . . . yes?"

Davy took a deep breath. Then he marched over and lifted the gate, just an inch, just for a second. Then he let go and let the gate slam down.

He gestured to the air next to him. "Ta-da!"

"Wow!" Jules exclaimed, and Finn clapped his hands.

"Your spirit isn't so shy after all," Runa said. "He's actually super brave!"

Davy stood a little straighter. "Thanks! I—"

Scritch-scratch.

He glanced at the gate, then hurried away.

The last event of Spirit Day was capture the flag. Once the group had walked to the town square, Principal King divided them into two teams. Nia was captain of a team with Quincy, Talise, Earl Grey, and their spirits. Davy was captain of a team with Jules, Runa, Finn, and their spirits.

Principal King handed Nia a turquoise flag with red polka dots. Then she handed Davy a lime-green flag with pink stripes.

"As captains, you have one minute to hide your flags," she announced. "Starting now!"

Nia sprinted in one direction. Davy took off in the opposite direction. He headed straight for the mermaid statue and tucked the flag between her fingers, which were holding a bronze dog collar. Then he hurried back to his team.

"Jules, you're in charge of guarding the statue from Nia's team," he said, panting. "Finn, Runa, and I will spread out and look for their flag."

"And our spirits will look, too, right?" Runa asked.

"Er, right," Davy said.

"Ready?" Principal King said. "Go!"

The kids scattered. Across the square, Nia's team scattered, too.

Davy kept an eye on Nia as he searched outside the library, then the post office. He'd nearly reached the comic-book store when he heard a scream! Startled, he turned to look—but it was only the barbershop pole. It spun and screamed whenever somebody got a haircut.

Just then, Nia dashed past Jules and headed straight for the mermaid statue. She was going to get their flag! Davy wanted to stop her—but then he looked at the screaming barber pole again.

It was blur of red and white . . . and *turquoise*.

"Aha!" Davy yelled.

He ran toward the pole as fast as he could, even though Nia was almost to the mermaid statue. There was no way he could beat her. . . .

He reached the barbershop pole just as it stopped spinning. The flag was gone.

Confused, Davy spun around to find Nia waving his team's green-and-pink flag. Principal King blew her whistle.

"That was a close one," she said. "But the winner is . . . Davy's team!"

Davy felt even more confused. "What? I didn't get the flag! I thought it was tied to the barbershop pole."

"It was!" Nia said, brow furrowed. "If you didn't get it, who did?"

"Who else?" Principal King pointed. "Davy's spirit, of course!"

The turquoise-and-red flag fluttered down at Davy's feet. Nia sighed gustily. "Oh, *well*. Congratulations, Davy!"

Davy blink-blinked, staring from the flag to Nia to the flag again. Did he really have a spirit after all? His team seemed to think so.

"We won!" Finn cheered, and Jules hooted, and Runa hugged Davy, and his spirit cartwheeled around the square.

Or at least, he was pretty sure it did.

Story 3:

Finn Gone Feral

Finn was going to be late for school.

The day had started out like every other, with Runa stopping by Finn's house so they could walk to school together. "Your girlfriend's here," Finn's third-oldest brother called.

"Runa isn't my girlfriend," Finn called back, like he did every morning. "I'll be ready in a minute!"

But that morning, getting ready took a lot longer than a minute.

First, Finn's third-oldest brother took so long shaving, Finn *almost* considered leaving for school without brushing his teeth. But only almost. He knew dental hygiene was very important, especially when you have a sweet tooth.

"You didn't even have any facial hair to start with," Finn grumbled.

In response, his third-oldest brother ruffled up Finn's auburn hair so messily, Finn had to spend twice as long fixing it.

Then, he couldn't find his math essay. He searched high and low. In fact, he was starting to consider searching even lower—in the basement—when his oldest brother admitted he'd used it as a coaster for his seaweed protein shake.

"What in the world is a math essay, anyway?" his oldest brother asked.

"Ms. Grimalkin was trying something different," Finn said, stuffing the damp paper into his backpack.

Ready at last, he hurried to the front door. But the porch was empty.

"Sorry, buddy," his second-oldest brother said. "Your girlfriend left for school without you."

"Runa isn't my girlfriend," Finn said. "I do think she's the coolest, most fascinating person in the whole entire world. But I don't feel that way about her. . . ."

He explained for a minute and a half before he realized his second-oldest brother had already left for school, too.

"Older brothers are so time-consuming," Finn said, checking his watch. *Uh-oh.* The tardy bell would ring in twelve minutes. It usually took Finn and Runa seventeen minutes to walk to school.

He was *definitely* going to be late.

Finn started jogging. He only made it half a block before he slowed, panting. Runa had often reassured Finn that he possessed many great qualities, but they both had to admit that athleticism wasn't among them.

"I need a shortcut," he said. Then he gulped.

The only shortcut Finn knew was through the beach forest.

None of the kids in Topsea spent much time in the beach forest. There could be anything hiding in those big, dense evergreens. Pirates. Dragons. Actual trolls (unlike Billy, the nice old woman who lived under the boardwalk). Runa swore she'd been searching for pinecones in the beach forest one evening, and way up high in one of the trees, she'd seen a kid with sticks and leaves in his hair, and he started howling at the full moon—

"The feral child!" Finn had gasped.

Runa had nodded. "Clearly, he was raised by wolves."

They'd both giggled. Wolves, like dogs, were mythological creatures. Therefore, feral children couldn't be real. Right?

Finn wasn't sure, but he hurried through the trees as fast as he could. Even though the sun was out, the beach forest seemed dark and shadowy. He had to keep zigzagging around tree trunks and ducking to avoid low-hanging branches. After a few minutes, he stopped.

"Where am I?" he asked out loud.

"You're in the beach forest," a voice replied.

Finn spun around.

A boy stood behind him. He was like nobody Finn had ever seen. He was barefoot. His white-blond hair was long and disheveled, and there were a few sticks and leaves in it. His skin looked suntanned, but he might have just been dirty.

The feral child was real!

Finn cleared his throat. He always spoke politely, but since he had a very small voice, he tried to speak loudly, too. "Yes! I know I'm in the beach forest! Thank you very much!"

"Why are you yelling?" the feral child asked. "I'm right beside you."

"Sorry," Finn said in an equally polite but quieter voice.

The feral child chuckled. Finn noticed his left eye was a deep, stormy green—exactly like the underside of a pine needle. But his right eye was a bright, pale blue—exactly like the wolf eyes Finn had seen in storybooks.

"What I meant was," Finn continued, "I don't know where I am *within* the beach forest. I'm lost."

"Maybe you're right where you're supposed to be."

"I'm supposed to be at school." Finn paused. "Do you even go to school?"

"I prefer not to."

Finn started to lose a little patience. "Going to school isn't a matter of preference," he tried to explain. "It's like, your official job as a kid or something."

"It's still a choice," the feral child said.

"Not according to my mom and dad," Finn said. "It's different with you, since you had wolves for parents."

"I had who for what, now?"

Finn wondered if the feral child's parents were a touchy subject. They shouldn't be! Finn's classmates had many different kinds of parents: single parents, double moms, stepdads, long-lost grandfathers. Although they were all human, as far as Finn knew.

"Um, never mind," he said. "But you live here? In the beach forest?"

"I live everywhere I am," the feral child replied. "But the forest is where I feel the most alive."

"For someone who doesn't go to school, you have a way with words."

The feral child smirked. "Well, I read quite a bit."

"Where do you get books?"

"The library."

Finn glanced at the feral child's feet. "Do you put on shoes when you go?"

"I prefer not to."

"Wow." Finn didn't love wearing shoes. He liked to feel the grass between his toes. He wondered how the floor of the library would feel under his bare feet. "That sounds kind of nice, actually. Do you howl at the moon?"

"Do you?" the feral child asked.

Finn giggled. "No!"

"Why not?"

"I don't know! It just seems kind of silly."

"Lots of things seem silly until you try them," the feral child said. "And then you find out they're actually super fun."

"Like what kinds of things?" Finn asked.

"I'd be happy to show you." The feral child winked his blue eye. "Unless there's someplace you're supposed to be?"

Finn thought about it a moment. "I guess since I'm already late . . ."

They both grinned.

The day had started out like every other. But it turned into one of the best days of Finn's life. The feral child made him a crown out of sticks and flowers to match his. They ate blackberries and flossed with blades of grass. After Finn kicked off his shoes, they went rock-hopping through a cool, bubbling brook.

"Watch out for brook blobs!" the feral child called.

"Are those like sea blobs?" Finn called back.

"Sort of. Brook blobs have teeth."

They ducked under a waterfall into a cave. It smelled suspiciously smoky, so they roared at each other like dragons and skedaddled. They used spiky pinecones to knock down purple oranges that stained their teeth when they ate them.

"Don't worry," the feral child said, grinning purplishly. "It'll only last a few days."

They climbed the feral child's favorite tree, one of the tallest in the entire beach forest. From its highest branches, Finn could see so much! He saw the seaweed-cracker factory and Hanger Cliffs Water Park, which had closed due to crab infestation before it had even opened. He saw the bluffs and the beach and the ocean.

"Wow, you can almost see the end of the endless pier," Finn said.

"Almost," the feral child agreed.

Finn could see the boardwalk, where Billy lived. The high school where his oldest and second-oldest brothers went to school, and the junior high where his third-oldest brother went to school.

And there was Topsea School! Finn saw the entire playground, including the jungle gym that looked just like the masts of a pirate ship. The cafeteria, where Nicky and Ricky and Micky dished up clam chowder and fried clams and clammed fries. (Before the clam shortage, anyway.) When Finn squinted, he thought he even saw Earl Grey waiting outside for Nia. The way Runa had waited for Finn this morning.

"I wonder what Runa is up to right now," he wondered out loud.

"Who's Runa?" asked the feral child.

"Runa isn't my—" Finn started to say automatically, then caught himself. Only his brothers teased him about Runa being his girlfriend. "Runa is my best friend," he went on. "I think she's the coolest, most fascinating person in the whole entire world, and—"

"FINN!"

The voice echoed through Topsea. "Who's Finn?" asked the feral child.

"Me!" Finn said. "I'm Finn. The voice sounds like my second-oldest brother. He's probably looking for me, since I never showed up at school. . . ."

"How many brothers do you have?"

"Too many! They're very time-consuming." Finn sighed. "But I'd better go find him."

The feral child nodded. "Yes, you'd better."

Finn glanced down. The ground looked very far below. "Could you help me climb down from here, please?"

For a moment, he thought the feral child might say, *I prefer not to.* But the feral child just smiled and nodded. "Of course."

The feral child guided him down the tree, then through the beach forest. Finn could hear all three of his brothers calling now. Right at the edge of the tree line, the feral child stopped. "I prefer to stay right here."

"I understand," Finn said.

They looked at each other.

Finally, Finn removed his crown of sticks and flowers and stuck it in his backpack. "Maybe sometime I'll get lost again," he said. "I think you're pretty cool and fascinating."

"You're pretty cool and fascinating yourself," the feral child said, winking his green eye.

Finn blushed.

Then he ran to join his brothers.

* * *

Later that evening, Finn looked out his window.

There was a full moon outside.

He sniffled. Maybe he was getting a cold? He rubbed his nose and gazed at the moon. It seemed to gaze back at him, almost playfully. Like a great big eye in the sky, if the other eye was winking.

Finn put on his crown of sticks and flowers.

Then he lifted the window, leaned outside, and howled.

"AROOOOO!"

He listened. For a moment, the night sounded like every other.

And then, way off in the beach forest, somebody howled back.

Talise

Story 4:

Whatever Floats Your Boat!

Typically, Talise spent Saturday mornings with the ocean. Sometimes she studied tides or examined tide pools. Other times, she put on her wet suit and flippers and buoyancy vest and everything else and went for a dive in the deep sea— just not the *deep*-deep sea, since she wasn't allowed to dive that deep without a buddy.

But the ocean had told Talise to build a boat. So today, she wanted to go to the boat supply shop.

First, Talise had to ask her parents. Fortunately, she was quite fluent in their dialect: Loving/Concerned, usually with a dash of Mystified. She started with her mother, who worked as a consultant. That meant people paid her for expert advice.

"I have never built a boat before, and I am feeling apprehensive," Talise said. "I would like to *consult* an *expert*."

She turned to her father, who worked as a controller. That meant he controlled . . . Talise wasn't entirely sure.

"I think that will help me take *control* of the situation," she continued. "Along with some boatbuilding supplies, of course. I'll just need you to accompany me with your credit card—"

"Talise," her mom said. She had white skin and dark blond hair. "But we had something else in mind for today."

"We know you've been spending a lot of time by yourself lately," Talise's father said. He had dark brown skin and black hair.

"Lately?" Talise repeated.

"Especially since Clara is visiting Puerto Rico for the next few weeks," her mother said. "So we arranged for you to spend the day with Runa!"

"*Runa?*"

Perhaps Talise looked as upset on the outside as she felt on the inside, because her father patted her shoulder. "She'll meet you at the pier. I'm sure you'll have a great time!"

Talise was not so sure.

She squeezed her sea blob as she walked to the beach. She'd really been looking forward to visiting the boat supply shop! Or at the very least, spending more time with her boat schematic. Instead, she was stuck with Runa, the kid Talise had the *least* in common with.

"She wouldn't be interested in boat supplies," Talise muttered.

The air was approximately 71 degrees Fahrenheit, while the ocean was closer to 58 degrees. She'd nearly reached the endless pier when something caught her eye. Her feet tripped, her heart skipped, and she stumbled to a halt, staring at the familiar collection of odd bubbles.

Wiggling her fingers, Talise stuck her hand into the pleasantly mucky sand and grabbed something hard. She wrapped her fingers around it and tugged.

SHLERPP!!!

It was another bottle, even crustier than the first one. Talise pulled out the cork and coughed at the musty smell. She shook out a rolled-up piece of very thin paper, or maybe it was tree bark.

The ocean had sent her another message!

Like the first message, this one had writing on it. Some words were blurry, but a few were legible.

Talise pictured the first message the ocean had sent her. *Hull*, she thought. *Engine. Luff. Maybe propeller. And this one says b—*

"*BOOM?!*"

Talise turned to find Runa standing behind her. "Oh, hullo," Talise said.

"You found another message! But why does it say *boom*? Was there an explosion? Once, I saw an explosion at the fireworks factory, and this one sparkler shot all the way up to the moon and nearly blew it to pieces. . . ."

"I don't think that's what *boom* means in this context," Talise said.

"Then what does it mean?"

Talise tried to explain, even though she still wasn't sure of Runa's dialect—was it Lively/Whimsical? Or maybe Upbeat/ Batty? "On a boat, a boom is a pole that helps control the angle of a sail," she said. "I believe this is a boat schematic—like a diagram."

Runa tilted her head. "Ooh, you're right! It's all smeary and blurry, like a watercolor painting."

"Something like that." Talise rolled up the message and tucked it into her pocket, then buried the empty bottle back in the sand. Her heart was still pounding. The ocean must *really* want her to build this boat.

"Hey, isn't that Quincy?"

Runa pointed down the beach, to where Quincy knelt in the sand with a pail. His parents and little sister, Roxy, sat on a blanket nearby.

The girls walked over to join him. "Are you collecting shells?" Talise asked.

"So far I've only found teeth." Quincy rummaged around in the pail he was holding. "Like this wisdom tooth!"

"Ooh, it looks extra wise," Runa said. "But you'll never guess what Talise found! Another—"

"BARNACLE," Talise yelled.

Then she winced. That was one reason Talise was no good at lying—anytime she tried, she had trouble controlling the volume of her voice. Runa gave her a questioning look. But fortunately, she said nothing.

"Um, barnacles are pretty exciting," Quincy said. "Roxy found a really old conch shell earlier."

They glanced at Roxy, who was gnawing on the end of something large and white.

"Roxy's been very interested in conchology lately," Quincy's mother said.

Roxy grinned, then blew into the small end of the shell. The *honk* made everyone giggle.

"Or maybe she's interested in the physics of sound," said Quincy's second mother. "Like me."

Both his parents were scientists, which Talise found very impressive. One was from Nigeria. The other was from Los Angeles. They both had dark skin, like Quincy and Roxy and Talise's father.

"Perhaps she is interested in bathymetry," Talise said.

The whole family smiled at her. "She does love tide pools," Quincy said, ruffling his little sister's hair. "And they've been extra interesting lately, with so much really old stuff washing up."

"That's true," his mother agreed. "The last time that happened was right before a Wildcard Tide."

Both Quincy and Roxy shuddered.

"We don't like Wildcard Tides," Quincy confessed. "Or any unpredictable tides, really. Hey, want to collect more teeth with me?"

"SORRY, WE—" Talise cleared her throat. "Sorry, we are unable to, but thank you for the invitation."

"That's okay," Quincy said. He and his family waved goodbye.

The girls continued down the beach. "Talise, slow down," Runa said. "What's the matter? Are you mad at Quincy?"

"No, I like Quincy," Talise said.

"Then why didn't you want to collect teeth with him? Or show him the message you found?"

"Because . . ."

Talise frowned. She didn't want to tell a lie. Not only was Talise no good at lying, it also made her very uncomfortable.

But other things made Talise even more uncomfortable. Like Jules rolling her eyes at Talise's boatbuilding book. Like her parents worrying about her being lonely. Like the entire class staring at her when she found the first bottle and announced that the ocean wanted her to build a boat.

"I would like to analyze this message further," Talise said. It was the truth, just not the entire truth. "Before I show it to anyone else. Is that okay?"

Runa smiled. "Are you asking me to keep a secret?"

"Well, yes. I suppose I am." Talise cleared her throat. "Runa, I would like to go to the boatbuilding store. And I would like that to be a secret, too."

"Absolutely!" Runa said. "You know, my little sister Lina told me a great secret a few weeks ago. She went to the fridge to get a snack, and when she opened the cheese drawer, all the cheese was *glowing.* . . ."

Talise half listened as they walked. Was Runa's dialect Fun/Quirky? Or Joyful/Flaky? It took so much energy to determine what was true and what was a lie—or a story—that Talise gave up and squeezed her sea blob instead.

"Oh, look, there's the dentist's office," Runa was saying. "I could use a checkup—I've had a really bad sweet tooth lately. The other day, my clam chowder tasted like a bowl full of sugar! Of course, my mom had substituted clam-shaped marshmallows for clams. Some were conch-shell-shaped, and a few were saber-tooth-shaped. . . ."

Talise wasn't even half listening now. Barnacle-covered bottles, conch shells, saber teeth—all kinds of old, peculiar items had been washing up on the beach. *The last time that happened was right before a Wildcard Tide,* Quincy's mother had said.

That made Talise feel a little worried. The wrong kind of tide would really mess up her boatbuilding plans!

The girls reached the town square. Talise's eyes went straight to one sign.

Whatever Floats Your Boat!

But Runa's eyes went straight to the shop next door. Or rather, the shaggy-haired boy walking inside.

"Davy!" she shouted, pulling Talise along with her.

Davy turned. His cheeks turned pink. "Oh, hi, Runa. Hi, Talise."

"Hello," Talise said. She couldn't help glancing at the boat supply store again. Unfortunately, Davy noticed.

"Are you here to get supplies for your—" he began.

"COMIC BOOKS," she shouted. A nearby flock of seagulls took flight, scattering mail all over the square. "We're here to buy COMIC BOOKS. I love COMIC BOOKS. I'm sorry for shouting, but I love them so much that I can't help it."

Davy blink-blinked. "Really? I mean, I love them, too, but I thought—"

"Me three!" Runa cut him off. "They're stories and art combined. My two favorite things. Shall we go inside?"

As she passed Talise, she gave her a great big wink.

Talise felt relieved. Runa's dialect might be confusing, but at least she was good at keeping secrets.

Inside the comic-book store, Davy and Runa immediately started browsing. Talise pretended to browse, too. But really, she was thinking about the tides again. As a very skilled diver, Talise didn't feel worried. But as a very unskilled boatbuilder, she felt *very* worried.

"Ooh, this one looks scary." Runa held up a comic book called *The Haunted Mini-Golf Course*. The cover featured a picture of a clown's face. His mouth was a door, and his tongue was a ramp for golf balls.

Talise did not think it looked particularly scary. Most mini-golf courses had a clown obstacle of some sort.

"That's almost as creepy-looking as the prize booth in the arcade!" Davy said.

Runa smiled. "Your spirit would probably be the only one brave enough to go in there, too."

Davy smiled back. But when Runa wandered to a display of pop-up books on Cubism, Talise saw his smile fade. In fact, Davy's expression did not match his dialect at all. His dialect was Brave/Eager, as usual. But his expression was Worried/Guilty.

"What's wrong?" she asked.

Davy blink-blinked. Then he blurted out: "I shouldn't have won Spirit Day."

"Why?" Talise asked. "Your spirit got Nia's flag first. Principal King saw it."

"I lied about having a spirit," Davy said glumly. "Spirit Day at my old school didn't include actual spirits. I couldn't find one—I didn't even know where to look! So I pretended to have a spirit, just to fit in."

Just to fit in. Talise studied Davy's face. He looked sad now, and a little embarrassed. She'd always thought Davy had learned Topsea's language really quickly. But apparently sometimes, he was only pretending to speak it.

"Fake it till you make it," Talise said.

"Huh?"

"It's an expression Clara told me once. It means that sometimes, if you pretend to know what you're doing, you'll feel more confident. And then you'll really be able to do it."

"Oh." Davy sighed. "Well, I faked it, but I didn't make it."

"Actually, I believe you did," Talise said. "Your spirit captured the flag, after all. Principal King saw it."

"You think that was really my spirit?" he asked hopefully.

"Of course. It was your first Spirit Day. Your spirit found you."

"Wow, thanks, Talise!" Davy's dialect was no longer Worried/Guilty. It was back to Brave/Eager. Talise felt pleased with herself.

They paid for their comic books (somehow, Talise ended up with two copies of *The Haunted Mini-Golf Course*) and said goodbye to Davy. At long last, Talise and Runa walked next door to Whatever Floats Your Boat.

The name of the shop had always bothered Talise. *Water* floated a boat, obviously. Not *whatever*!

Now it made her feel optimistic. So did the second sign, written on a thin piece of tree bark:

We Sell: Hatches, Booms, Jibs, Hulls, Engines, Luffs, Propellers, Masts, and More!

But then she saw the third sign, hastily scrawled on a thick piece of paper:

Closed Today

For Boat Repair Emergencies, Please Send a Request by Express Seagull

Talise's optimism was replaced by impatience. "Drat," she said.

"*Request by Express Seagull,*" Runa read. "I saw one of those once! It was a really colorful seagull, almost like a parrot, all blue and red and yellow and green and—"

"But I don't have a have a boat repair emergency," Talise said. "I don't even have a boat yet."

"You will," Runa said. "And yours definitely won't sink!"

"Hmm," Talise said.

The ocean had told her not once, but *twice*, to build a boat. That's what she intended to do. But even skilled, experienced boatbuilders who had read all the library's books on boatbuilding failed sometimes.

If Talise tried to fake it, she definitely wouldn't make it.

She squeezed her sea blob.

THE TOPSEA
SCHOOL GAZETTE

WORD OF THE DAY

Schematic (n.): A simple sketch that shows you how something is built.

LIGHTHOUSE KEEPER ON VACATION?

by Jules, Fifth-Grade Star Reporter

Thanks to a pair of super-powerful, super-expensive bird-watching binoculars, the *Gazette* can report with confidence that the lighthouse is still completely empty. According to this reporter's stepsister, the first stage in a missing person investigation is to interview people close to the missing person. So this reporter headed to the beach, where the clam boats have been running up on the rocks. Is the lighthouse keeper to blame for Topsea's continuing clam shortage?

"Of *course* the lighthouse keeper is to blame for Topsea's

continuing clam shortage," said Gaspard, a clam boater this reporter found duct-taping the bottom of his boat. "Everyone knows night's the best time to hunt clams. Well, without any light from the lighthouse, how am I expected to see these rocks? She picked a rotten time to take off work!"

According to Gaspard, this isn't the first time the lighthouse keeper has vacationed.

"She took one about a decade ago or so," Gaspard said, shooing a few rock cats away from his net. "Wasn't gone for this long, though. Look at this, would you? This net should be crammed full of clams. Instead, I've got canines and buckteeth and bags of oolong tea. All sorts of peculiar things." He paused, untangling a tusk from his long, gray beard. "When peculiar things start washing up like this, that's a sign something BIG is coming."

This reporter knows better than to doubt the wisdom of someone with such a long beard. But the lighthouse keeper is usually very responsible, and it seems unlikely she would take an extra-long vacation and leave the clam boaters high and dry. This reporter vows to uncover the truth. That is, as soon as she's ungrounded for borrowing her father's binoculars without his permission.

NURSE'S NOTES

Listen up, kids: the flu is going around Topsea. Symptoms are often unpredictable and may include stuffy nose, fever, and fiery sneezes. This virus comes on very quickly, and it clears up within a few hours. Teachers are advised to stock their classrooms with tissues and fire extinguishers.

Stay healthy,

Nurse Xavier

THE POETRY CORNER

Seasonal seaweed

Seems silly, or even sad

Sometimes sinister

—Davy

CAFETERIA MENU

~ MONDAY ~

Snack

Orange Smiles and Lemon Frowns

Lunch

~~Clamburgers~~* and Fries with ~~Clam~~ Chowder*

~ TUESDAY ~

Snack

String Cheese or Yogurt Yarn

Lunch

SHH! It's a Surprise!

~ WEDNESDAY ~

Snack

Grapes

Lunch

Yam Fritters and ~~Clam~~ Fritters*, Mystery Meat

~ THURSDAY ~

Snack

Pigs-in-a-Blanket with Seaweed Ketchup

Lunch

Baked Beans or Bacon Beans or Baked Bacon (with Beans)

due to the clam shortage, all clam entrées will be replaced with the student's choice of ham or "clam," a tofu-based clam substitute

~ FRIDAY ~

Snack

Chocolate Milk or Chocolate Tea

Lunch

Corn Dogs and Cats with Stewed Spinach

Nia

Story 5:

Food Fight

Nia whistled as she headed to the cafeteria. Earl Grey trotted at her side, squealing along. Their duet was more beautiful than the greatest symphony the universe had ever heard. (That's how it felt to Nia, anyway.)

Then Nia's whistle became a cough. Then her cough became a groan.

"Uuuugggghhhhhh," she groaned.

"Uuuugggghhhhhh," Earl Grey snorted.

"You too, huh?" Nurse Xavier stood at the cafeteria entrance, bald head gleaming. He put a hand to Nia's forehead, then Earl Grey's. Then he marked something on his clipboard.

"What's going on?" Nia asked. "We felt fine a minute ago, and now we have the *plague*."

Nurse Xavier chuckled. "Not the plague. The flu."

"That's even worse! Should we go home and drink tea?" Nia patted Earl Grey. He attempted to wag his tail, but the teacup was too heavy.

"Nope!" Nurse Xavier replied. "Most Topsea students have the flu this morning. Fortunately, this virus has a very short cycle, and should be gone by this afternoon. It's best that you all stay right here, so your families don't catch it, too."

"Okay. Thanks, Nurse Xavier."

With a heavy sigh, Nia trudged into the cafeteria. Earl Grey plodded along behind her. She slumped down in a chair, dropped her backpack onto the floor, and thunked her head on the table.

"No one in the history of the entire world has ever felt as terrible as I do right now," she announced.

Nia wasn't only the most competitive kid at Topsea School. She was also the most dramatic. She couldn't *help* it—all her emotions spiraled and sparked like firecrackers in her chest. (That's how it felt to Nia, anyway. Although maybe it was her cough this time?)

But today she had real competition. All of her friends looked just as terrible as she felt!

"I doe wad you bean," said Quincy. His nose was red and stuffy. "By dose is wed add stuppy. Id feels like id bight fall off!"

"I have a splitting headache," Talise told them. "Figuratively.

65

As you can see, my head is still in one piece. It just feels split. Like driftwood after it's sawed in half for—"

"KOO-HWAH! KOO-*HWAH*!"

Nia and her friends jumped, startled. Finn pressed a napkin to his mouth. "Sorry!" he said. His crown of sticks and leaves slipped sideways.

"That's the loudest cough I've ever heard!" Runa rubbed her pink, watery eyes, clearly impressed. "Where *did* you get that crown, anyway?"

"Um, I made it," Finn said.

Nia noticed Jules's mouth was moving, but no sound seemed to be coming out. "Did you say something, Jules?"

Jules heaved an enormous sigh. Then she pointed to her throat with her spoon, crossed her eyes, and stuck out her tongue.

As her best friend, Nia understood immediately. "Jules has a sore throat and lost her voice," she informed the others. "Wow. I guess the flu really is going around Topsea!"

Across the table, Davy squirmed uncomfortably. "Is it? I don't have any symptoms."

"You might have some and you just don't know it yet," Talise said. "According to Nurse Xavier, the symptoms of this particular flu can be unpredictable."

"Udpredicdable?" Quincy repeated. "Oh doh."

"Are you sure you don't have *any* symptoms, Davy?" Nia asked. "Even Earl Grey has the chills."

She pointed under the table, where Earl Grey was wrapped in an extra-thick, extra-scratchy blanket. Nanny must have

66

packed it that morning. It was almost as if she had known Nia and Earl Grey were going to get sick today! Nanny did have a second sense for things like that.

Nia sniffled. She wished she was home right now.

"Aw, Earl Grey looks so warm and snuggly," Runa said. Then she squinted. "Oh, wait, I was looking at Davy's shoes."

Quincy pulled a bag of graham crackers and marshmallows from his lunch box. "Wad are your sybtobs, Dia?"

Nia put on her bravest, most long-suffering face. "I feel like I haven't slept in ten years. My muscles hurt like I just ran twenty miles. And my temperature is at least thirty billion degrees!" She slumped back in her chair, arms dangling. "And I'm *starving*. Nanny always makes me the best soup when I'm sick."

"You can get some soup in the soup line," Runa suggested.

The soup line was all the way on the other side of the cafeteria, which might as well have been an island across a vast ocean. "I wish I could just summon a bowl of chowder," Nia said.

CLANG!

"Look out!" yelled Ricky as the kitchen door flew open. Something small and white zoomed over him. It sailed across the cafeteria—right toward Nia! She gasped and covered her head.

Thunk. "Ow!"

Nia peered through her fingers. A bowl sat upside down on Davy's head, and chowder drip-dropped down his face.

"Was that for me?" she asked.

Davy wiped a chunk of potato out of his eye. He opened his mouth, then paused, blinking furiously.

"Ah . . . ah . . . *ahhhh* . . . *CHOO!*"

Sparks shot out of Davy's nose, roasting Quincy's marsh-mallows. "Fire!" Runa yelped, grabbing her chocolate milk and tossing it in Talise's face.

"There's no fire," Talise sputtered. "Only smoke."

"Where there's smoke, there's fire," Finn pointed out. "Usually. But this time . . . uh-oh."

Jules was flapping her hand in front of her face frantically, her eyes wide.

"AHHH-*CHOOO!*"

Flames flew from her mouth and onto the pile of smoky marshmallows. Everyone gasped and stood up, backing away from the blaze. The cafeteria doors opened, and Nurse Xavier stepped inside. "Is something on fire?"

"We need water!"

"No, we need napkins!"

"No, we need chocolate!"

"Duck!"

"Why would we need a duck?"

"No, *duck*!"

Everyone ducked as a whirlwind of napkins and bottles of chocolate syrup sailed out of the kitchen, along with a stream of water from the sinks. It flew right over the kids—and into Nurse Xavier's face!

Nia cringed. "Oops."

"You kids have the *flu*," Nurse Xavier said, wiping chocolate syrup off his bald head. "You should be resting, not food fighting. Now I need a shower!"

The cafeteria doors slammed shut behind him.

"Food fighting?" Ricky demanded, hands on his hips.

"It's not what it looks like," Nia said.

"Then why is food flying all over the place?"

"Telekinesis!" Runa exclaimed.

"Tele*what*?"

"Telekinesis. It's when you can control objects with your mind. I think so, anyway. One time, Madame Flea's fortune said she controlled the arcade games with her telekinetic powers—"

"You mean I summoned the chowder with my *mind*?" Nia asked. "I don't know, Runa. That's pretty far-fetched, even for you."

Jules rolled her eyes. Finn furrowed his brow. Ricky scratched the fork-and-knife tattoo on his left bicep.

But Talise nodded thoughtfully. "I think Runa might be right."

"You do?" Runa looked more surprised than anyone.

"It makes sense," Talise went on. "Nia just said she wished she could summon a bowl of chowder, and then she did. Telekinesis as a flu symptom is the most obvious conclusion."

"Nurse Xavier *did* say the symptoms are unpredictable," Finn said.

"Oh doh," said Quincy anxiously.

"Oh *yes*," Nia said, warming up to the idea. "I can totally control things with my mind!"

Davy shook his head, sprinkling everyone with chowder. "So you *were* trying to start a food fight."

"Is that true, Nia?" Ricky asked sternly. "This is quite a mess!"

It was the greatest injustice to ever happen at Topsea School. (That's how it felt to Nia, anyway.) "It wasn't on purpose!" Nia insisted. "Why would I throw chowder at Davy?"

Davy raised his eyebrows. "Revenge for winning Spirit Day?"

Nia made a face. Payback hadn't been her plan—but maybe it wasn't a bad idea. Especially if she had telekinetic powers!

"Come on, Davy," she said. "If it'd been on purpose, I wouldn't waste something as delicious as chowder. I'd . . . I'd dump a hundred bottles of seaweed ketchup on your head!"

An eerie silence fell over the cafeteria.

Nia felt a tingling behind her eyes. Suddenly:

WHOOOSH!

Like a flock of seagulls, a hundred bottles of seaweed ketchup flew over the hot lunch line in a V-formation. They headed straight for Davy, who yelled and covered his head with his arms. The bottles flipped over and shook, dousing Davy and everything around him in thick, green ketchup.

"By barshballows!" Quincy exclaimed.

"My french fries!" Runa popped a few ketchup-covered fries in her mouth. "Mmm, delicious."

As for Davy, he looked like the giant green blob in a cheesy old horror movie Nia had watched once with Nanny. Two brown eyes blinked at her from behind the green slime. Nia couldn't help it. She started giggling.

The brown eyes narrowed. Then they closed.

"Uh-oh," Nia said.

"Hang on, now." Ricky stared at Davy. "What are you—"

Clatter-CRASH!

Nia looked around for a place to hide, but the massive tub flying toward her was quicker. It flipped over—and started to rain mystery meat. "Ew, carnitas!" she shrieked, flapping her arms. "Or beef! Or goat! Whatever it is, make it stop!"

"Get a mop!"

"Get some clue sauce!"

"KOO-*HWAHHH*!"

Finally, the empty tub clattered onto the floor. The green blob laughed.

Nia scowled, brushing chunks of ground-up mystery meat off her shoulders. Then she squeezed her eyes closed, ignoring Ricky's howls of protest.

WHOOOSH!

"Surprise!" Nia yelled. The green blob gasped just as a fishy-smelling casserole flew into his face with a *smack*.

"That Surprising Tuna was supposed to be a surprise!" Ricky grumbled. "Oh, wait . . . I guess it was."

Nia climbed on her chair and raised her arms. "I'm the food fight champi—*argh!*" she sputtered as something stinky and sticky splashed her from head to toe. A large pot clanged to the floor in front of her. Stewed spinach hung from Nia's braid, from her nose, from her ears.

Now *she* looked like the green blob.

She started laughing. So did Davy. From under the table, Earl Grey let out an amused snort. Even Quincy giggled nervously. Soon everyone was laughing.

Everyone except Ricky.

As soon as Nia saw his expression, she stopped giggling.

Nanny got the same look after Nia let Earl Grey splash in mud puddles on his evening walk. Splashing was fun for Nia and Earl Grey—but muddy girl-and-hog prints tracked through the house weren't any fun for Nanny.

"Who's going to clean up this mess?" Ricky wailed. "Cosmo is still putting out snot fires in the kindergarten classroom. And what about all this wasted food? We'll need a whole new menu for the rest of the week!"

Quincy's hand shot up. "I'll do it! I love to cook."

"It's probably not sanitary to cook with a stuffy nose," Talise pointed out.

"But he don't sound stuffy anymore," Jules said. Then she beamed. "And my throat isn't sore! I can talk!"

Ricky tapped his foot impatiently. "I'm glad you're all feeling better, but what about this mess? And the menu?"

"Nia and I started the food fight," Davy said. "So we'll help with the new menu. And we'll clean up, too."

"We will?" Nia said.

"It's only fair." Davy drip-dropped green ketchup as he walked to the mop and bucket in the corner.

She hated to admit it, but Davy had a good point. Because Nia's parents traveled a lot, Nanny did most of the cooking and cleaning. It's not as if Nia didn't help *at all* . . . but she could probably be more helpful. Especially because she liked Nanny. And Ricky, too.

"I think we should make hot dogs for tomorrow's lunch," Davy told Nia as she wiped the tables. "And chili. My mom and I make *really* spicy chili."

"Oh yeah?" said Nia. "Because Nanny and I make the spici-
est carne asada in the *world*. Way spicier than any chili."

Davy stopped mopping and grinned at Nia. "Wanna bet?"

Nia grinned back. "You're on."

CAFETERIA MENU

~ MONDAY ~

Snack

Orange Smiles and Lemon Frowns

Lunch

~~Clamburgers*~~ and Fries with ~~Clam~~ Chowder*

~ TUESDAY (Revised) ~

Snack

String Cheese or Yogurt Yarn

Lunch

~~SHH! It's a Surprise!~~ Hot Dogs and Davy's Very Spicy Chili

~ WEDNESDAY (Revised) ~

Snack

Grapes

Lunch

Yam Fritters and ~~Clam Fritters*~~,

Nia's Very *Very* Spicy Carne Asada (Way Spicier Than Davy's Chili!)

~ THURSDAY (Revised) ~

Snack

~~Pigs-in-a-Blanket with Seaweed Ketchup~~

Chiles Rellenos Stuffed with Oatmeal

*due to the clam shortage, all clam entrées will be replaced with the
student's choice of ham or "clam," a tofu-based clam substitute*

Lunch

Baked Beans or Bacon Beans or Baked Bacon (with Beans)

~ FRIDAY (Revised) ~

Snack

~~Chocolate Milk or Chocolate Tea~~ Earl Grey Tea and Extra-Fancy Biscuits

Lunch

Corn Dogs and Cats with ~~Stewed Spinach~~ Spirit Stew

(Invisible but Definitely Real and Very Nutritious!)

**thanks to Guest Chefs Nia and Davy for helping out

with this revised menu!

Story 6:

Color and Beauty and Glitter

Runa was going to be late for school.

"I know that's unusual," Runa told Finn on the phone. "I still feel bad for leaving without you last time! But my eyesight's been blurry ever since I got over the flu, so my dad's driving me to the ophthalmologist. That's a doctor who makes sure your eyeballs aren't falling out—"

"It's okay," Finn said.

"Really?"

"Of course. A little change might be good for me, you know?"

Runa hung up, feeling mildly bewildered. Finn *hated*

walking to school alone. That was why she stopped by his house every morning, even though it wasn't exactly on the way. Did Finn have another friend he was walking with?

That'd be okay, of course. It's not like Finn was Runa's boyfriend—they didn't feel that way about each other, and never would! Anyway, Runa had other friends, too. Like Talise. Even though they had wildly different interests, they'd had fun hanging out the other day. They even shared a secret!

But Runa still felt a little funny.

"Still feeling funny, Runa?" her dad asked as they drove down Main Street. It was blurry.

"She *looks* funny," said her little sister, Lina, who was in second grade.

"I'm sure the ophthalmologist will fix you up in no time."

"If not, maybe it'll help my art," Runa said bravely. "The great Impressionist painter Claude Monet had cataracts later in life."

"Oh, that's why his paintings were so squishy-looking!" her dad said.

"You'll be good at painting sea blobs," Lina said.

Runa sniffed. "Philistines."

At the ophthalmologist's office, Runa's dad tried on glasses to make them giggle. "How about these?" he said, wearing tortoiseshell frames exactly like Ms. Grimalkin's.

The ophthalmologist walked in. "Eyeglasses aren't toys, young man," she said to Runa's dad, then winked at Runa and Lina. They giggled harder.

"Sorry," Runa's dad said sheepishly.

First, the ophthalmologist had Runa look through a machine with her left eye and name the images she saw. "Dragon, clamcake, table, orangutan, sea orb, jack-o'-lantern, comic book, buffalo." Runa laughed. "One time my grandparents came to visit from South Korea, and we visited an island where a bunch of wild buffalo lived, and they were all the descendants of Hollywood movie stars—"

"Now your right eye," the ophthalmologist said.

Obediently, Runa peered into the machine. She hesitated. "Potato?"

"Mm-hm. I see."

"Is there flu in my eyeball?"

The ophthalmologist twisted some knobs, then shook her head. "Potato."

"Huh?"

"More specifically, mashed potato, or possibly a fleck of french fry." She winked again. "Get into any food fights lately?"

"Um . . ." Runa replied.

"I'm going to put some drops in your eyes. They should take care of the problem shortly—although they might make you see a little differently for the rest of the day."

Runa took a deep breath, then opened her eyes wide. The last thing she saw was a green glob, which looked a little too much like seaweed ketchup. "Ack," she said pleasantly.

"How is your eyesight now?" the ophthalmologist asked.

Runa crossed her eyes, then peered into the machine again. She still saw a potato—but now it glowed bright blue. "Ooh, much prettier."

"Perfect," the ophthalmologist said. She glowed bright blue, too.

Runa joined her dad and sister in the waiting room. Both of them glowed!

Her dad's glow was more of a milky tan, though. And Lina glowed a milky yellow.

"How in the world did you get potato in your eye?" Lina exclaimed.

"Um . . ." Runa replied.

"All that matters is you're feeling better," her dad said. "After Lina's checkup, I could really go for a cup of coffee. With extra creamer."

"Yuck," said Lina. "Make mine a banana milk!"

"Hmm," Runa said.

As they drove through town, Runa couldn't believe her eyes. Topsea was prettier than it'd ever been. She already saw color and beauty and glitter in places the other kids didn't see. But now it was even easier!

Everybody she saw glowed different colors. Bright ones, dull ones, lively ones. And it wasn't just people who glowed, but other things, too. Seaweed glowed a ticklish-looking turquoise. After Runa's dad dropped her off at school, she noticed the jungle gym shone shimmery gold, as if something was buried underneath.

Runa stepped inside the classroom, then froze.

"You're all so *beautiful*," she said.

Davy giggled. "Thanks!"

"How was the ophthalmologist?" Ms. Grimalkin asked. Her

glow was stripy, bright, and soft-looking, like rock kitten fur with the sun shining on it.

"She put drops in my eyes." Runa fell into the nearest empty seat, which was beside Talise. "My vision isn't blurry anymore. But now I'm pretty sure I can see everybody's *auras*!"

"What's an aura?" Nia asked, scratching her neck.

"I'm not really sure," Runa admitted. "But one time, my grandmother told me *her* grandmother could see auras, and that was how she fell in love with my great-great-grandfather, because his aura was the prettiest one she'd ever seen. Anyway, there's a unique, colorful glow around each and every one of you—"

"Suuure," Jules said.

Runa sighed. "I'm not telling tales! I swear. Jules, your

aura is really bright. And it's not just still—it's flashing."

Jules perked up a bit. "Tell me more."

"It's kind of hard to describe. I wish I could show you, but then you'd have to go to the ophthalmologist, too—and anyway, I'm not even sure a person can see their own aura. . . ." She glanced down at herself. "Oh, wait. Sparkly!"

Finn giggled. Runa smiled at him.

Then she frowned. Everybody's auras were different, but Finn's aura looked sort of . . . *exceptionally* different.

"You're quite skilled at painting, Runa," Talise said. "Why don't you paint the auras so our classmates can see them?"

"That's a great idea!" Runa said, surprised. She knew art was Talise's least favorite subject, so it was kind of her to suggest it.

At recess, Runa brought out her colored pencils and watercolors and oil pastels and clay and charcoal and an easel. Her classmates and Earl Grey crowded around her as she painted Jules's aura in flashing shades of copper and silver.

Suddenly Runa realized Talise wasn't with them. She spotted her over by the jungle gym, measuring it with a complicated-looking tool. "Talise!" she called. "Come here, I'm painting auras!"

Talise looked a little surprised, but she walked over to join the other kids.

"I hope that tool has nothing to do with boatbuilding," Jules said.

"IT HAS NOTH—" Talise shut up when Runa elbowed her.

"Why do you care whether Talise is building a boat or not?"

Runa asked Jules. "She's allowed to have different interests. No need to make her feel silly."

"Sure, but—I'm just *saying* that factually, building a boat based on one washed-up old message makes no sense—"

"Well, maybe you don't have *all* the facts," Runa said, thinking of Talise's secret second bottle.

There was a moment of awkward silence. Runa hoped she hadn't said something wrong again. It wouldn't be the first time. As usual, it was hard to read Talise's feelings, although she appeared to be squeezing something in her hand.

But Jules's cheeks were red. "I'm sorry if I made you feel silly, Talise."

"I don't feel silly," Talise said. "But thank you. Your aura is very pretty. The flashing copper and silver reminds me of the lighthouse."

Jules brightened. "How funny! I was just thinking about the lighthouse."

Runa was glad nobody seemed to be fighting anymore. "Whose aura should I paint next?" she asked.

"Mine!" Finn said, straightening his crown of sticks and leaves.

Her stomach sank. Finn was Runa's best friend, but she felt confused by his aura. "Actually . . . I'm feeling inspired by Quincy's aura."

She painted it with dollops of strawberry pink, chocolate brown, and vanilla white, layering it on as thick as frosting.

"Yummy," Quincy said.

"It does resemble a baked good," Talise observed.

"Now Davy's!" Runa rifled through her art supply bag. "I'm going to need a lot of spray glitter—it's even sparklier than mine."

"Interesting," Talise said once Runa had finished. "Your auras are complementary."

"Maybe Runa could start an aura matchmaking business," Nia said, scratching her knee.

Davy's aura blushed.

"Is it my turn now?" Finn asked.

"No, me!" Nia exclaimed. "I need to know my aura is flashier than Jules's."

Runa studied Nia's aura. It was a beautiful color—but it also looked gritty. Kind of scratchy, actually. She blended together several pink sunset hues, then grabbed a handful of sand and sprinkled it on top.

"Hmm," Nia said, scratching the back of her ankle with her other foot.

"Why are you so itchy?" Quincy asked.

"I was a couple days late on Earl Grey's flea pill. I think a few must have bit me." Nia threw an apologetic glance at Earl Grey, who was currently itching his hind end on Runa's easel. "What does his aura look like?"

"Even scratchier!" Runa said.

"Fascinating," Talise said. "It's as if auras reflect our thoughts at any given moment. Or perhaps what we're thinking about the most."

Runa wasn't too sure about that—otherwise, how could she explain how odd Finn's aura looked?

She picked up her brush. She set it down again. "Sorry,

Finn," she said. "Maybe my eyeball is malfunctioning or something . . . but I'm not sure how to paint your aura."

"But you can paint anything!" Finn said.

"True," Runa said. "It's just—it might take a while. What time is it?"

"Could you describe it instead?" Talise suggested. "That's what I do in my logbooks. There is rarely art involved, unless I'm sketching plans for my—you know." She squeezed the thing in her hand again. It appeared to be a sea blob, but that didn't make any sense.

Runa relented. "All right. The top part is blue-green. Like the color of wolf eyes in storybooks mixed with the underside of a pine needle."

Finn's eyes widened. "Um, that sounds . . . pretty."

"It is! But the thing is, there's also like, a weird haze of dirt around your feet. Like a big dirty cloud of dirty dirt."

"Did you just call Finn's aura dirty?" Jules asked.

Finn turned pink.

"Just the foot part! Like someone aimed a fan at his feet, after he'd been walking barefoot in the woods or something. . . ."

"There's nothing wrong with that," Finn said.

"I didn't say there was!" Runa said, but he'd already hurried away, clutching his crown of sticks and leaves.

She sighed. Boys could be so *sensitive*.

But then, girls could be, too. After the bell rang, Talise stuck around to help Runa gather her art supplies. "Do you think I should have lied about Finn's aura?" Runa asked. "I'm afraid I hurt his feelings."

"As you know, I am no good at lying," Talise said. "You, however, lie quite easily."

"Hey!"

"But if auras *do* reflect our thoughts, Finn likely would have known."

"That's true." Runa sighed. "But why was he thinking about the *forest*? Finn's my best friend—he never keeps secrets from me."

"Did you tell him about the second bottle I found?" Talise asked.

"Of course not!" Runa exclaimed, offended. Then she paused. "Oh, I see what you mean. I guess he'll tell me when he's ready."

"And when my boat is ready, I won't mind if you tell Finn about the bottle."

"Deal!" Runa stuffed the last of her art supplies into her bag. "You know, I never got the chance to paint your aura."

Talise shrugged. "That's okay. Maybe just describe it to me?"

"It's an easy one," Runa said. "Your aura looks like the ocean."

They both beamed.

From

EVERYTHING ELSE YOU NEED TO KNOW ABOUT TOPSEA

by Fox & Coats

Moon Phases

In most places, the tides are predictable. That's because they follow the moon. But in Topsea, the tides are hard to predict. The moon has a mind of its own.

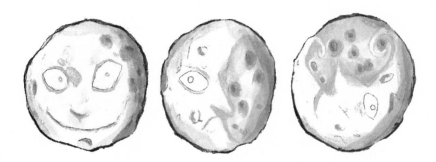

Playful Moon

Often, the moon feels playful.

It winks at you from the night sky. Or the daytime sky.

It bounces around, playing hard to get. It's in the treetops. It's behind the clouds. It's even in that mud puddle. Don't splash! Great, now there's mud and moon all over both of us.

Full Moon

When the moon is full, its eyes are wide open.

Ever notice how it follows you as you walk?

Maybe sometimes you walk a little faster. After a while, you glance over your shoulder to see if the moon is still there. It almost always is.

It even follows you when you run.

Lonely Moon

Sometimes, the moon feels lonely.

But it's a strong, independent moon, and it makes its own friends. It breaks its reflection into bits and pieces so they can splash in the rippling waves.

Half-Moon

A half-moon means the other half is hiding somewhere. (Have you checked your cheese drawer lately?)

Quarter-Moon

A quarter-moon is enough for a gumball. Unless you want one of the big gumballs. Then you'll need two quarters.

Crescent Moon

If you happen to find a crescent moon, don't pick it up. The pointy ends are sharp.

Blue Moon

On rare occasions when the moon is low-spirited, town spirit is inexplicably high.

New Moon

Sometimes, when you glance over your shoulder, the moon isn't there at all.

At first, you might feel relieved. Nobody likes to be followed, unless they've told you it's okay. (If they haven't, you should probably stop immediately.)

After a while, you might start wondering what the moon is up to.

We wish we could tell you.

But it's a secret.

Story 7:

Sea Apes

When learning how to do something, it can be just as helpful to learn what *not* to do.

"Like laundry," Clara had told Talise once. "Never put a red sock in with your white shirts! Unless you want pink shirts."

Talise did not want pink shirts. Therefore, in order for Talise to build a boat that would float, she needed to study boats that *couldn't*—like shipwrecks. And the only logical way to study shipwrecks was for Talise to visit them herself.

Problem was, most shipwrecks were located in the *deep-*deep sea—and Talise wasn't allowed to dive in the *deep*-deep sea without a dive buddy.

"I don't mind diving alone," she told her parents over break-fast. "Or working alone. I'm even building a boat without any assistance."

"Hey!" her father objected. "Didn't we order you all those boatbuilding tools?"

"And we helped you collect that enormous pile of wood," her mother said. "I still have splinters!"

"Have you tried extracting them with a very fine fishbone?" Talise asked. "That's what Ms. Grimalkin uses. I can search for one when I'm investigating shipwrecks—"

"No deep-deep dives without a buddy," her father said firmly.

Talise poked at her "clam" omelet. It didn't squeak, unlike her rubber-duck omelet the other day. "But some of the shipwrecks aren't even *that* deep-deep. Just two or three hun-dred feet."

Her father shuddered. "That's where the seaweed *grows*."

"It grows all kinds of places. There was even some growing in my extra-deep soaking bathtub." Talise paused. "You know, extra-deep isn't that different from deep-deep—"

"Talise," her mother said.

"Why don't you talk to your friends?" her father suggested. "I'm sure one of them would be interested in getting a scuba license."

Talise set down her fork and squeezed her sea blob. She'd talked about scuba diving plenty of times. Her classmates seemed to like the *idea* of it:

"Sea stars? Psychedelic eels? All kinds of anemones? Wow."

"Self-Contained Underwater Breathing Apparatus sounds like the name of a killer robot!"

"You're saying there might even be mermaids *down there?"*

But once they learned that getting an actual license took a lot of work, they quickly lost interest. Talise found that hard to understand. Diving was what she loved most in the world, other than the ocean itself!

And her mother and father, of course.

(Though maybe she'd love them the *teeniest* bit more if they'd dive with her.)

Talise walked to the beach with her hands in her pockets, squeezing her sea blob. She went straight to the pile of wood her parents had helped her gather, along with her boatbuilding tools and supplies.

Her poor boat. She'd barely started building it, and already there could be an engineering flaw that would send it sinking to the deepest, darkest places at the very bottom of the ocean. And Talise along with it.

At least that would get her underwater. . . .

"Wait," she said out loud.

Her parents hadn't specified that her diving buddy had to be *underwater*, had they?

A little while later, Talise was standing beside Runa on the endless pier. Runa wore a yellow jumpsuit with inkblots all over it. Talise wore flippers and an air tank and a regulator and a BCD and all her other scuba gear.

"I'm so flattered you asked me to be your buddy!" Runa said

happily. "I mean, I already *knew* we were buddies. But a dive buddy—wow! That seems like a big deal."

Talise nodded. "Especially since we have nothing in common."

"What? That's not true."

"I would have yelled if I was lying."

Runa giggled. "I'm just saying, you're mistaken. We have a *secret* in common, don't we?"

It was true. Maybe that was why Runa had seemed like the obvious choice? Even though Talise still hadn't figured out her dialect. Right now it seemed like Enthusiastic/Slightly Confused, but that could change at any moment.

"What do I have to do, exactly?" Runa asked.

"Just stand right here while I dive," Talise said. "Or you can sit, if you'd prefer."

"Ooh, lots of options."

"I've mapped out the shipwrecks I'll be exploring in here." Talise held up her copy of *Abandon Ship! A Guide to Exploring the Deep-Deep Seas of Topsea*. "I'll be underwater for approximately an hour."

Runa gazed into the water. "How will you know *where* to come up? This pier's pretty long, if you haven't noticed. Endless, actually. I heard about this one kid who wanted to try to find the ending of it, so she started running and running—"

"Because of the mussels," Talise explained.

"Huh?"

"That's how I'll know where to come up. There's a more muscular collection of mussels on this pillar than any of the others.

There's also a seal family who keeps this part of the kelp forest trimmed."

Runa squealed. "A seal family? Maybe I *do* want to learn how to dive!"

Talise's insides filled with relief. "Oh, good. If you look in my dive bag, you'll find the first two volumes of bookwork under my spare BCD. I've highlighted the most important passages—"

"What's a BCD? Is it your fancy vest?"

"Indeed. Rather, my Buoyancy Control Device. It inflates to help you float on the surface of the water. It also affixes your dive tank to—"

"Oof," Runa said. "Honestly . . . I don't think diving is for me. It seems like too much gear! All I need to draw is a pencil and paper."

"All I need to dive is myself," Talise said. "But with flippers and an air tank and a regulator and a BCD and all my other scuba gear, I can go much deeper and stay underwater much longer."

Runa sighed. "It'd be so much easier if you had a magic ring or something!"

Talise rolled her eyes. Then she popped her regulator into her mouth and jumped off the edge of the pier.

SPLASH!

When she surfaced, she inflated her BCD.

WHOOOSH!

"I think I get it!" Runa knelt at the edge of the pier. "All your gear is like art supplies. Sure, I can draw with just a pencil. But with colored pencils and watercolors and oil pastels and clay and charcoal and spray glitter, I can make much better art."

Talise popped her regulator out of her mouth. "What exactly *is* spray glitter, anyway?"

"It's glitter in a spray bottle," Runa replied.

"Oh. I thought there was more to it." Talise popped her regulator back into her mouth.

"Are you sure you'll be okay?

Talise popped her regulator out of her mouth. "Yes. I'm a very experienced scuba diver. My parents should trust me to dive as deep as I want."

"Wait—how deep are you diving?"

"My license is for deep-sea diving. I'm just going to go a little *deeper* than deep today." Talise was careful to tell the truth, since Runa would know if she was lying.

"Do your parents know?" Runa sounded nervous. Which made Talise feel nervous, too.

"YES!" she yelled. "Oops, sorry. Yes, my parents know that I'm licensed to dive in the deep sea. I plan to go a little deeper than deep today, which should be OKAY—*ahem*—because I have a dive buddy."

"That's me," Runa said.

Talise pressed the button to deflate her BCD.

HIIIIISSSSS.

"I'll see you in one hour!" Runa called, waving both hands. "Let me know if you see any mer—"

Talise slipped under the ocean's surface.

All her nervousness faded instantly. The temperature of the water was 61 degrees, but Talise felt perfectly warm in her wet suit. As she descended, she paused every now and then to pinch her mask's nosepiece and clear her ears so her eyeballs didn't explode.

That wasn't a very good joke.

Down, down, down she went. A pod of sugar snap squid zoomed past her mask. Talise smiled on the inside. (But only because it was difficult to smile on the outside with a regulator in her mouth.) Clouds of tiny sea apes went bananas. They were like sea monkeys, except they didn't have tails. Talise's insides smiled wider. Technically, Talise was a sea ape as well.

That was a better joke! She wondered if it would make Runa laugh.

Talise checked her depth gauge: deep, but not *deep*-deep yet—although it was deeper than she'd gone in a long time.

Using her compass, she swam toward the first shipwreck. This one was a motorboat—which made it a motorboatwreck. Judging by the chunk of coral still wedged in its side, it had failed due to coral reef collision. Talise would be sure not to make that mistake.

To make sure, Talise peered inside. An eye looked back at her. "Blorpp!" she exclaimed.

Luckily, it was a big, googly eye, not the rubber duck kind. An octopus burst from the motorboatwreck, then swam to another chunk of coral and froze. Its googly eye goggled at Talise. If the octopus could speak, it would probably lie. "I AM NOT AN OCTOPUS," it would say. "I AM A CORAL."

Talise giggled. Runa was really missing out!

According to her dive watch, it had been nineteen minutes.

Talise descended even deeper . . . Then *deep*-deeper. When she was at the correct *depth*-depth, she swam toward the second shipwreck from the map in her guidebook.

This one was a pirate ship. The sails had long since rotted away, but there were still plenty of cannons. Talise counted thirty-seven of them. Cannons were very heavy. So were cannon-balls. She counted 216 of them.

Whether the ship had failed due to weight or pirate war, Talise wouldn't make those silly mistakes, either. She didn't intend to put any cannons on her boat. Well, maybe one cannon, if there was room.

She sat on an old, rotting trunk filled with coins and checked her dive watch. It had been forty-one minutes.

Drat. She was running out of time!

Getting to the surface safely took quite a while. But she *really* wanted to see the third shipwreck—the deepest one of all.

Talise descended even *deep*-deeper.

At last, she reached the seaweed forest. It was dark and gloomy and cold. And the current was much stronger than Talise had expected. She kept needing to grab stalks of seaweed to steady herself. A couple times, they grabbed back.

She started to feel nervous again. She didn't see the ship-wreck *Abandon Ship!* had promised. And peculiar items kept whizzing by her face. Some looked like teeth. Others looked like dentures. (One looked like a rubber duck.)

What was going on?

Talise had been worried about a Wildcard Tide messing up her boatbuilding plans. But this felt different. This felt much

bigger, and stronger. She wanted to investigate further—but then she checked her dive watch.

It had been fifty-eight minutes.

"*Blaaaaaargh,*" she sighed into her regulator. Her bubbles startled a miniature sea serpent, who rocketed away. "Blarry," she apologized.

She hoped Runa wouldn't mind waiting a little longer. There was no way Talise could get to the surface safely in two minutes.

As soon as Talise reached the pillar with the most muscular mussels, she began to swim toward the surface. She swam very, very slowly. It's important to ascend very, very slowly to avoid getting the bends, which is when nitrogen bubbles form in a diver's body and migrate to dangerous places.

Usually, surfacing was the worst part of every dive. Talise always wished she could stay underwater forever.

But for the first time, she was eager to get back to land.

First, she was armed with new knowledge of nautical failures: that they were often for silly reasons. Second, she wanted to consult her moon and tide charts as soon as possible.

Most of all, she couldn't wait to tell Runa about all the marine creatures she'd seen on her dive. Sea serpents. Cannonballs. Sugar snap squid. A mermaid—

Talise blinked behind her mask. For a second, she thought she'd glimpsed a flash of fin and dark hair.

But that was impossible.

She checked her dive watch again. Uh-oh. It had been seventy-four minutes. She was very, very late.

The ocean grew warmer and brighter. Finally, her face broke

the surface. She inflated her BCD, which really was a fancy kind of vest.

WHOOOSH!

Talise lifted her mask onto her forehead. "Runa, I apolo—" she began, then stopped as she realized Runa wasn't alone.

"Talise! What were you thinking!?"

Talise's mother and father stood beside Runa. They looked worried. They looked angry.

And Runa looked very, very guilty.

TALISE'S LOGBOOK

Name: Talise Villepreux

Date: Sunday

Location: Endless pier

Time in: 12:30 **Time out:** 14 minutes too late ☹

Bottom Time: 1:28

Depth: DEEP-deep!

Temperature: 54°F

Visibility: Initially excellent, then dark and gloomy

Observations:

This dive was extremely helpful for my boatbuilding endeavor. Or rather, it should have been. Because I went deep-deep diving without a buddy, I am grounded and unable to work on my boat. Logbook, I find this extremely unfair.

I also did not manage to locate the shipwreck in the deep-deep ocean. Perhaps the current moved it to another location? Lots of peculiar items were swirling around, too. Almost as if the ocean was trying to warn me about something . . .

According to Jules's reports in the *Gazette*, I am not the only one who believes something is on its way. I would like to discuss it further, but I know she thinks my boatbuilding endeavor is a waste of time. (Even if she is nicer about it now.)

I suppose there is one bright side to being grounded: now I have plenty of time to consult my moon and tide charts.

THE TOPSEA
SCHOOL GAZETTE

Today's Tide: Very Low

Today's Forecast: Local meteorologists are reporting that love is in the air.

WORD OF THE DAY

Philistine (n.): Someone who makes no attempt to truly understand or appreciate the arts.

THE LIGHTHOUSE KEEPER HAS RETURNED!

by Jules, Fifth-Grade Star Reporter

An exciting development in the ongoing lighthouse investigation: the lighthouse keeper is back! She was first spotted in the lighthouse tower yesterday just after sunset—although it's possible she's been back longer and her appearance went unnoticed, as even the most vigilant reporters have lots of homework to do.

But something is still not right. Late last night, the lighthouse began flashing all the colors of the rainbow. While the impromptu dance party on the beach seemed fun, this reporter would like to remind everyone that a lighthouse flashes lights as a WARNING. But the clam boats are all still being repaired, and there are no ships in sight. So who is the lighthouse keeper trying to warn? And what is the warning about? Something BIG, perhaps?

Sadly, the lighthouse keeper hasn't left the lighthouse for questioning. But this reporter vows to get her attention—even if it takes marine signal flares.

MESSAGE FROM THE PTA PRESIDENT

This is a reminder to all students that boatbuilding is dangerous and should be avoided. Working with wood can give you splinters, and working with tools of any sort is highly discouraged. If you are in need of a boat, please go to the boat rental shop by the docks, which has been closed indefinitely because boats are dangerous and should be avoided.

Story 8:

A Love Story

E arl Grey had a heart full of love.

He was a very large watch hog. So he had a very large heart.

Like he did every morning, Earl Grey gazed at Nia while she slept. Nia was Earl Grey's all-time favorite Nia. His love for her was as big as the sun, which was shining through their bedroom's big bay window.

At last, Nia woke up.

"Earl Grey! I've told you, it's a little creepy when you do that." Nia hugged him around the neck, then opened the curtains. "Wow, what a *beautiful* day!"

She tied a yellow ribbon on Earl Grey's very curly tail.

After Nia got ready for school, she and Earl Grey raced down the spiral staircase. They rocketed into the kitchen, where Nanny was watching telenovelas on a giant screen. Currently, two fancy-looking people were smooching.

"Ack ew ick!" Nia exclaimed. "I hate the kissy ones."

"¡Cállate, mija!" Nanny said affectionately. "They're madly in love."

Earl Grey wrinkled his snout. He'd never been *in love*, madly or otherwise. But he did love Nanny, his all-time favorite Nanny. She made chiles rellenos stuffed with oatmeal instead of seaweed. She never, ever made bacon for breakfast.

Nanny tapped the giant screen. It switched to two even fancier people: Nia's parents.

"Good morning, Mama and Papa!" Nia exclaimed.

"¡Buenos días, mija!" Nia's parents beamed from their satellite office in Mexico City. They traveled a lot for their family's international real estate business. Sometimes Nia went with them during school vacations. Earl Grey was thankful that didn't happen too often, since he didn't have a passport yet.

¡Buenos morning! he exclaimed. It came out "Snuffle-snuff," but Nia's parents seemed to understand.

Once they hung up, Nanny kissed Nia's forehead. Then she patted Earl Grey's backside. "Largarse, cerdito tonto."

Understanding Spanish took Earl Grey a little extra effort, but he'd been studying hard so he could travel to Mexico City with Nia. So while he was pretty sure Nanny's words translated to "Scram, silly piglet," he knew she'd *really* meant *See you later, my all-time favorite piglet.*

Earl Grey trotted alongside Nia as she walked to school. Some days, he went to class with her and listened to Ms. Grimalkin's lessons. Ms. Grimalkin was Earl Grey's all-time favorite teacher, even if her fingernails were sharp. After Earl Grey had saved the cafeteria's milk from the mean-toothed rockycats, she'd even rewarded him with a watch-hog-size cushion to sit on.

But on sunny days like today, Earl Grey preferred to take a stroll and say hi to all his other favorites.

Like any honorable watch hog, he kept an eye out for anybody's day that needed saving. Danger occurred less frequently on sunny days, but Earl Grey was always prepared.

As he passed Hanger Cliffs Water Park, he stopped and stuck his snout through the gate. He hoped they'd reopen soon. Jules, who was Nia's all-time favorite best friend forever (besides Earl Grey, obviously), had said the Hanger Cliffs engineers were busy designing an inner tube large enough to fit watch hogs. Apparently, nobody had informed them watch hogs float just fine on their own.

Earl Grey withdrew his snout, then smiled as two crabs scuttled crookedly past. Since crabs tend to look a lot alike, he wasn't sure they were his all-time favorite crabs. But they definitely weren't spiders.

Good días, Earl Grey began.

Then he paused. It looked like the crabs' claws were hooked together! Uh-oh—were they *stuck*?

Earl Grey lifted his snout to the sky and sounded the alarm: *HWEEE! HWEEE! HWEEE!*

Then he trotted over to help. His snout wasn't as dexterous

as a hand full of fingers, but still managed to unhook their claws.

"Snort!" he said in triumph.

Immediately the crabs hooked their claws together again.

"Snort?" Earl Grey asked in confusion.

"*Clackity-click-click clack,*" said the crabs.

Understanding Crabbish took Earl Grey a little extra effort, but he was pretty sure it translated to "Scram, we're madly in love." The crabs weren't stuck—they were holding claws.

Earl Grey congratulated them on their madness and walked away, still feeling a little confused. But he was happy for the love-crabs, really.

As he passed the beach forest, he heard a loud ruckus over-head. Before he could figure out where it was coming from, something bonked him on the head.

"*Oink!*" he oinked.

It was a package wrapped in brown paper. Earl Grey's very large heart fluttered. Was the package for him?

No, it was addressed to the Town Committee for Lunar Consequences. Then an envelope fell into the sand, addressed to the same place. Three more came to rest beside it—along with a white feather.

The ruckus grew louder. Earl Grey looked up and saw two seagulls perched in a tree, flapping their wings and squawking loudly at each other. The last of the mail they were supposed to be delivering tumbled to the ground. Uh-oh—were the seagulls *fighting*?

Earl Grey sounded the alarm:

HWEEE! HWEEE! HWEEE!

Startled silent, the seagulls squinted at Earl Grey. Then they flew over and landed in front of him. *"CAW,"* they said. *"Caw awk-caw."*

Understanding Gully took Earl Grey a little extra effort, just like Crabbish did. But he was pretty sure it translated to "Scram, we're madly in love." The seagulls hadn't been arguing—they'd been singing.

You call that singing? said Earl Grey. It came out "Squee-hee-hee," but the seagulls seemed to understand.

"Awk-caw-CAW," said one seagull, offended.

"Snoff," scoffed Earl Grey, equally offended. He wasn't jealous! He was happy for the lovegulls, really. Even if his heart was starting to feel a little funny.

He headed for the beach.

Due to Very Low Tide, the ocean was farther away than usual. Earl Grey admired the giant pile of logs and driftwood on the sand. Nia's classmate Talise had been gathering tree parts for the boat she wanted to build.

Earl Grey loved boats. Maybe Talise could use some help?

She was in class, though, and he wouldn't want to start without her. Also, Talise had never *asked* for help. But then again, Earl Grey knew that not everyone asks for help when they needed it—

"MROW!"

Earl Grey skidded to a stop. He'd been so distracted, he'd almost trotted straight into the rocks!

The mean-toothed rockycats didn't seem fond of Earl Grey. Actually, they didn't seem particularly fond of *anybody* in

Topsea. But ever since the milk-stealing incident, they'd glared at him a little harder. And they seemed to have more mean-teeth every time they smiled.

Particularly the pair of rockycats on the rocks in front of him. Their tails were swishing. Their yellow eyes were slits.

"Mrowwwwwrrr . . ."

Uh-oh—were they *growling*?

Earl Grey sounded the alarm:

HWEEE—

Then he stopped himself. The rockycats weren't even looking at him, he realized. They weren't growling. They were purring.

"Snore," Earl Grey said.

The rockycats purred harder. Their tails made a heart shape.

Earl Grey had no desire to learn Rockycat, but by now he could guess what they were saying: they were madly in love.

He was happy for the lovecats, really. But for some reason, he didn't *feel* happy anymore.

Earl Grey had always had a heart full of love, ever since he was a tiny piglet. But unlike the rockycats, the seagulls, the

crabs, and the fancy people on Nanny's telenovela, he'd never been *in love*. Not even with the stuffed narwhal Nia's friend Davy had won for him at the arcade.

Earl Grey had a heart full of heartache.

He was a very large watch hog. So his heart ached an awful lot.

Hanging his head, Earl Grey headed for the boardwalk. It was usually empty this time of day, and a lonely boardwalk seemed like the perfect place for an achy-hearted hog to wallow. But today, he saw somebody familiar sitting on one of the benches.

"What's the matter, mi cerdito tonto?" Nanny called. "Your tail is uncurled."

Earl Grey glanced back at his tail. It was true.

Nanny patted the bench. "Siéntate. Tell me your troubles."

He shuffled over and climbed onto Nanny's bench, trying to take up as little space as possible, which was almost all of it. He told her about the crabs, and the seagulls, and the mean-toothed rockycats. *I have all this love in my heart, and nobody to give it to*, he finished. It came out "Siiiiiiiigh," but Nanny seemed to understand.

"Love is in the air," she told him. "Literally. I read it in this morning's forecast."

Earl Grey had forgotten to check the forecast.

Nanny retied the yellow ribbon on Earl Grey's tail. "When everybody seems to be falling in love around you, it can make you feel a little lonely," she went on. "But why wallow in it? You're a strong, independent watch hog—and still a young watch hog, after all. And there's no shortage of love in your life. Or in your heart."

Earl Grey raised his eyebrows. Well, sort of. He didn't have eyebrows, but it was the thought that counted.

Nanny chuckled. "Think about it, cerdito mío. Why did you try to save the crabs and seagulls and rock cats?"

For fame and glory, Earl Grey said.

But then he thought about it. And he knew the real answer.

Because I love them, he said.

I love the clicky-clacky crabs with their claws hooked together. I love the squawky seagulls despite their unreliability when it comes to important packages. I even love the rock cats with their glow-in-the-dark eyes and their sharp, pointy fangs. I love everybody and everywhere and everything that ever was and everything that ever will be, but not even close to how much I love my best-beloved Nia, and you, my all-time favorite Nanny.

It came out "Oink!" but Nanny seemed to understand.

"I love you, too, cerdito mío."

Earl Grey smooshed his snout against Nanny's kneecap. And then, he heard another of his all-time favorite voices calling his all-time favorite words.

"Earl Grey!" Nia called.

"Squeeee!" Earl Grey replied.

"Earl—*Nanny?*" Nia came running down the boardwalk. She skidded to a stop. "Is anything wrong? I heard Earl Grey's alarm—"

"Everything is just fine, mija," Nanny said. "In fact, your watch hog saved the day three times today!"

113

Nia gasped. "Really?"

"Well, sort of. There were a few misunderstandings, but it's the thought that counts."

Nia wedged herself onto the remaining two inches of bench. "What are you doing on the boardwalk, anyway?"

"Enjoying a bit of sun," Nanny replied. "I just finished playing poker with Billy and Cosmo."

"Wait—did you say *poker*?"

"*¡Claro que sí!* What, you think I just cook and watch telenovelas all day?" Nanny tugged on Nia's braid. "Sometimes Xavier joins us on the weekends."

"*Nurse* Xavier?"

Nanny nodded. "He's a good friend. In fact, we're cowriting a book."

"That's so cool!" Nia hugged Nanny around the neck. Then she hugged Earl Grey.

I love you both as big as the sun, said Earl Grey. It came out "Snuffle-uffle," but Nia and Nanny seemed to understand.

Nia ran back to school, and Earl Grey and Nanny trotted home for lunch. Afterward, Nanny read him "This Little Piggy," a story Earl Grey wasn't too sure about. A pig would never eat roast beef! And he'd certainly never *wee-wee-weed* all the way home. (Well, maybe when he was a very little piggy.)

He loved the story anyway.

Maybe Earl Grey had never been *in love.* But he had a heart full of love and a belly full of oatmeal. And for now, that was all he needed.

He was still a young watch hog, after all.

JULES

Story 9:

Funny Hunches of Boats

Jules's stepsister, Hazel, was factually the best investigative reporter on the planet. So when Hazel came to visit for a few days, Jules felt positive she'd help her finally solve the mystery of the lighthouse keeper's warning.

"Sorry, Jules," Hazel said, pinning back her short red hair with a barrette. The barrette was a silver star, and matched her tiny nose ring. "I'd love to help you out, but I need to head to the library for some research."

Jules deflated. "What are you researching?"

"I'm in the middle of a fascinating investigation on the health benefits of seaweed. There's a lot of misinformation out there."

"Oh." It sounded boring. But if Hazel said it was fascinating...
then Jules knew it was *factually* fascinating.

"Hey, why don't you come to the library with me?" Hazel
asked. "A little research might help you crack this lighthouse
keeper case!"

"Sure, I guess." Research was Jules's least favorite part of
being a reporter. But if Hazel thought it was a good idea . . . then
it was *factually* a good idea.

The Topsea library was especially busy that afternoon. The
BOOK CHECKOUT line was long, and the PEOPLE CHECKOUT line was
even longer.

"I guess I'll start with books," Hazel said. "Although there's
a seaweed-factory worker whose brain I'd love to pick, if the
People Checkout line gets shorter."

"I'll start with books, too," Jules decided.

She followed Hazel to the head librarian's desk. Next to a
tall stack of books, she saw a nameplate that said *Chrissy Éclair.*
At first, Jules thought no one was at the desk. But then a head
popped up. The head had curly black hair, brown skin, and
extra-big eyes behind thick glasses with square-shaped yellow
frames. The head was also attached to a neck and a body.

Too bad, Jules thought. What a scoop that would've been:
How Topsea's Head Librarian Got Ahead with Only a Head!

"Hello!" said the head librarian's head. "How can I help you
today?"

"Hi, Ms. Éclair," Hazel said. "I was wondering where I
could find some books on the health benefits of seaweed."

"Please, call me Chrissy," the librarian said. "You'll find

117

what you need in the seaweed section upstairs—three rows down to your right."

Hazel headed for the stairs. Jules was about to follow when a book caught her eye. *"The Great Book of Boatbuilding,"* she said. "My friend Talise read this!"

Chrissy nodded. "Her mother returned it today."

Jules's stomach twisted. She knew Talise was grounded because she'd gone diving to study shipwrecks. Talise truly believed the message in a bottle she'd found was telling her to build a boat.

Factually, that still didn't make sense to Jules—but she did feel guilty about being so dismissive. After all, as a reporter, she understood the importance of following a hunch. She had a hunch that the lighthouse keeper was trying to warn the town about something. Talise had a hunch that she needed to build a boat.

Maybe their hunches had something in common.

"Can I help you find anything, Jules?" Chrissy asked.

"Oh!" Jules blinked. "Yes, please. I'm researching the lighthouse keeper. Do you have any books about her?"

"Hmm." Chrissy tapped her chin. "I believe we might have something in the biographies aisle. Right this way!"

Jules followed her past shelf after shelf. Each had a label:

COOKBOOKS

BAKEBOOKS

HISTORY

ALTERNATE HISTORY

POETRY (*For Spoken Word Poetry, Slam Poetry,

and Rap, Please Visit People Checkout)

FOREIGN LANGUAGES

LOCAL DIALECTS

BIOGRAPHIES

(*For Living Memoirs, Please Visit People Checkout)

"Here we are," Chrissy said. "Biographies are organized by profession, so we need to find the *Ls* . . . ah, here! Lawyer, Leather Belt Maker, Lexicographer, *Librarian!*" She pulled a thick book with a purple cover off the shelf.

"Is that your biography?" Jules asked.

Chrissy nodded proudly. "Took me years to write, but it was worth it. Just look at how many . . ." She trailed off as she flipped to the back. "Oh. Only two people have ever checked it out. Well, that's better than none!" Adjusting her glasses, she squinted. "Oh. That was me, both times."

Jules felt bad. "I'm sure it's a very good biography, but—"

"It is!" Chrissy wailed. "I spent all that time in the jungle, learning how to forage for paper. And I have a black belt in binding!"

"But I really need to research the lighthouse keeper today," Jules finished.

"I understand. Lighthouse keeping is a fascinating profession."

They kept moving down the row, past biographies for Lifeguards and Lightning Guards, Lion Tamers and Literary Agents, Lion Agents and Literary Tamers, Lockpicks and Locksmiths and Lock Mediators. . . .

"Wait," Jules said. "If there's a Lighthouse Keeper biography, we must have passed it."

"You're right." Chrissy took a few steps back, her fingers trailing along the tops of the books. Then she said, "Aha!" and slid a book off the shelf.

It had a pretty, shiny cover with a picture of a lighthouse. But there weren't that many pages. "It's so *thin*," Jules said.

"What's wrong with that?"

"Short books mean less information. I was hoping for *lots* of information."

"I see." Chrissy smiled. "I'll let you in on a little secret.

Sometimes thin, short books have *lots* to say. And sometimes big, long books don't have much of anything to say at all. This book might not have many words—but they could be the exact words you need."

Jules perked up. "That makes sense. Thanks, Chrissy!" Then she tilted her head. "Are your glasses . . . glowing?"

Chrissy pushed the yellow frames up her nose. "They are! Helps me read even when I don't have a light." She winked, and Jules decided they were factually the coolest glasses in the world.

Upstairs, Jules found Hazel at a table towering with thick, important-looking books, her star-pierced nose buried in *100*

Mostly True Facts About Seaweed. She looked the way an investigative reporter was supposed to look.

Compared to her stepsister, Jules felt foolish with her thin little book. She sat down across from Hazel and sighed loudly.

"What's wrong?" Hazel asked.

"Chrissy helped me find the lighthouse keeper's biography," Jules muttered.

"That's great!" Hazel buried her nose in the massive book again.

Jules slumped in her chair and glared at the biography. Finally, she opened it to the first page. Instead of words, there was a picture of a mermaid. She was small with long green hair, and wore a shell necklace.

On the second page, Jules found another picture of the mermaid. Her head poked up out of the water, and she stared longingly at a distant shore.

On the third page, the mermaid wore a glowing ring. The fourth page showed the mermaid walking onto shore with human legs. . . .

"I don't *believe* it!" Jules yelped, slamming the book shut.

"Jules," Hazel whispered. "You can't yelp in a library."

"Sorry. My point is, this isn't even the right book." Jules pulled off the book jacket with the picture of a lighthouse, revealing a plain cover that said *The Magic Ring.* "See? It has nothing to do with lighthouse keeping—it's just a silly story about a silly mermaid and a silly ring. It's *fiction.*"

"Not necessarily," Hazel said. "Mermaids really did exist."

"But it isn't helpful to my investigation at all."

"All I'm saying is, there's almost always truth in fiction. You might have to work a little harder to find it, but it could be in there."

Jules wrinkled her nose. "How am I supposed to do that?"

"First, you read the whole book," Hazel explained. "Then, you consider all of the facts about your case. Then, you look for connections."

Frowning, Jules opened the mermaid book again and forced herself to keep turning the pages. When she got to the part where the mermaid got her happily-ever-after—a peanut butter and pickle sandwich, which wasn't available in the ocean— Jules rolled her eyes so hard they crossed.

"It's like one of Runa's goofy stories," she muttered.

Maybe Hazel was right about finding truth in fiction sometimes—but now was not one of those times.

Jules was on the wrong track. Factually.

She gave up and headed downstairs, meandering aimlessly through the aisles. She followed a set of dirty footprints into the travel section, with books on all kinds of places outside of Topsea. She wandered through the wander section, with books on how to travel. She coasted into the isle aisle, with books on how to bury treasure.

When she rounded the last shelf, she found Chrissy unpacking a box of books. "Can I help you find something else?" the librarian asked.

"I don't think so." Jules stepped closer, furrowing her brow. "Is that box . . . *wet*?"

Chrissy flicked a piece of seaweed off the box. It wriggled

away down the row, disappearing into the bathymetry section. "Yes, this whole shipment of *Everything Else You Need to Know About Topsea* was six months late. The boat sank, can you believe it? Thankfully, the books were double-Bubble-Wrapped, so they aren't water damaged."

"How did they get here, if the boat sank?"

"They all washed up this morning, lucky for us!" Chrissy pulled another copy from the box, and a clump of wet sand landed in her lap. "Ick."

"But *how*?" Jules asked again.

The librarian shrugged. "Ask the ocean."

Ask the ocean.

Jules stared at the box. An urgent, funny sort of feeling flared in her middle, racing to her brain like a stick of dynamite.

"Gotta go; thanks, Chrissy!" she exclaimed. Then she sprinted back to her stepsister. "Hazel! *Hazel!*"

Hazel looked up, startled. "Are you okay? Were you in the ghost section?"

"No, listen—I think I had a breakthrough!"

"Tell me!" Hazel grinned. "I'm about done, anyway. I thought this book would be helpful because it's so big, but it seems like more of the same old seaweed propaganda."

"Okay." Jules took a deep breath. "According to Chrissy, a boat sank six months ago. But its shipment only washed up this morning. And tons of other stuff has been washing up, too—all those old bottles, and teeth, and other peculiar things. Gaspard, the clam boater I interviewed, said that means—"

"Something BIG is coming."

Jules beamed. "You read my report?"

"Of course! So the lighthouse keeper's warning involves something BIG—that makes sense. Do you know what it is?"

"I have a hunch, but . . ."

Jules trailed off. Her hunch was BIG. But it wasn't factual—not yet. As a responsible reporter, Jules had an obligation to prove her hunch was right before she sounded the alarm.

If she was right, her alarm wouldn't be the only one.

But if she was wrong . . . Jules could see the headlines now. *Hasty* Gazette *Reporter Harms Town with False Alarm!*

"But first," Jules continued, "I need to consult an expert."

Hazel laughed. "I respect that! What kind of expert?"

"One who knows more about the ocean than any kid in Topsea." Jules smiled. "And all the grown-ups, too."

THE TOPSEA
SCHOOL GAZETTE

Today's Tide: *Ominous*

WORD OF THE DAY

Nigh: (adj.)*:* very, very near

BREAKING NEWS: EXTREMELY HIGH TIDE IS COMING

by Jules, Fifth-Grade Star Reporter

This reporter thought she'd hit a wall on her investigation. After all, it's hard to learn about lighthouse keepers when their biographies are just silly mermaid books in disguise. But thanks to a soggy shipment of sunken books, this reporter finally figured out what the lighthouse keeper has been trying to warn us about.

You heard it here first, *Gazette* readers—an Extremely High Tide is nigh!

Of course, this reporter would never cry wolf unless a wolf was *factually* there. That's why she consulted with Topsea's leading bathymetry expert, Talise Villepreux. After studying her moon and tide charts extensively, Talise concluded that there is no doubt: the tides are turning in Topsea, in a BIG way.

Everyone in Topsea—with the exception of new students and stepsisters who just visit occasionally—knows Extremely High Tide is only dangerous if you don't follow safety protocol. The Town Committee for Lunar Consequences hasn't issued their standard preparation notifications yet, but this reporter is confident they will follow her lead and sound the alarm soon.

PRINCIPAL'S PRINCIPLES

Learning to work with tools is an important and fun part of any child's education. Students who wish to build things like tables, shelves, or even boats are encouraged to go for it! Whatever floats your boat.

Your Pal,

Principal Josephine (Jo) King

NOTIFICATION: THERE IS NO EXTREMELY HIGH TIDE

From the Town Committee for Lunar Consequences and Everything's Going to Be Okay

We are aware of the rumors that an Extremely High Tide might be on its way. Rumors are not news, and to report them as facts is very irresponsible. That type of propaganda can lead to panic and hysteria—all for nothing! According to our very reputable observations, razor-sharp analysis, and overly educated guessing, we assure you **an Extremely High Tide is NOT on its way**. If it was, you'd hear it from us first! Right? Don't worry! Be hungry. Bring this ad to Nico's Taqueria for 50% off on a "clam" quesadilla. Everything will be just fine.

Story 10:

Truth or Dare

Quincy woke up in a brand-new mood.

Between the unpredictable flu and all the talk about unpredictable tides, he'd felt especially anxious all week. As a result, he'd baked six pies, two dozen cookies, and a giant loaf of seaweed-banana bread.

But everyone had long since recovered from the flu. And despite the *Gazette*'s report, a committee of grown-up experts said an Extremely High Tide was *not* on its way. (By the time Quincy had seen the notification, he and Roxy had already strapped on a dozen life jackets each.)

(Quincy still slept with one on, just in case.)

This morning, all Quincy's anxiety had vanished. He didn't know the name of his new mood yet. But he liked it.

He also liked salted caramel swirl pancakes. As he started a batch, his crème brûlée torch suddenly sneezed a stream of flames onto his butter. Normally, Quincy would have panicked. But instead, he scooped up the butter with a pan and let it brown, then poured the pancake batter on top.

His parents were impressed with the result.

"Salted caramel swirl pancakes are good," his mom said around a mouthful. "But brown butter salted caramel swirl pancakes are *amazing*."

"You should take more risks with your recipes, Quincy!" his other mom agreed, pouring syrup onto her stack. "This is delicious."

After breakfast, he headed to the boardwalk to meet his friends.

Normally, Quincy walked with his head down. He wanted to make sure he didn't trip over a stick or a crack. But today, he kept his head up. Topsea was so pretty! Sometimes Quincy forgot. The ocean was so blue, and the sand was so sparkly, and the rock cats were so smiley.

Smiley—maybe *that* was the name for this mood?

Quincy smiled all the way to the boardwalk. When he saw Davy, Jules, Nia, and Earl Grey, he smiled even bigger. "Hi!" he called.

"Hi, Quincy!" Davy said. "Wow, you look different today. You look . . . merry!"

"No, he looks jolly!" Nia argued.

"Nah, he looks radiant!" Davy argued back.

"He looks buoyant!"

"Sunny!"

"Moony!"

Quincy giggled. He felt like all of those things. But Jules scowled. "Would you two stop bickering already?"

Nia put her hands on her hips. "Well, I'd rather bicker with my best friend, but all she can talk about is the Town Committee for Lunar Consequences and—"

"—and Everything's Going to Be a Disaster?" Jules finished. "They totally *ruined* my reputation as a reporter! They don't understand the definition of propaganda. And worst of all, they're *wrong*. Talise is way more of an expert than those guys, and she's *positive* an Extremely—"

"Hi, Runa!" Quincy bellowed, waving both hands. Everyone turned as Runa walked up, arms wrapped around her art supply bag. She didn't wave or smile.

"Where's Finn?" Nia asked.

"He's busy," Runa replied.

The other kids waited for her to tell them about Finn's plans to fly over the Bermuda Triangle, or go on a jungle safari, or an equally colorful Runa-tale. But she didn't say anything else.

"What about Talise?" Davy asked at last.

"She's been grounded all week," Jules reminded him. "That's why she's had so much time to consult her charts and confirm my hunch about Ext—"

"Extremely delicious clams," Davy cut in, glancing at Quincy.

131

Quincy just smiled. Davy didn't need to worry about him. There was no Extremely High Tide. Everything was fine. His cheeks ached.

"It also means Talise can't work on her boat!" Runa sniffled. "The whole reason she's grounded in the first place. She cared so much about building it, she put her entire life at risk in the deepest, darkest parts of the seaweed-infested ocean. . . ."

Quincy had never seen Runa look so gloomy. When he was worried about something, his parents always came up with a fun way to distract him.

"What would you like to do today, Runa?" he asked. "Maybe play a game?"

"I'm *not* in the mood for a game," Jules grumbled.

But Runa's face began to brighten. "Ooh, I like games. Which one?"

"Truth or Dare?" Davy suggested.

Truth or Dare usually made Quincy anxious. After all, it was an unpredictable game. Someone might ask him about his favorite crabcake recipe, or they might dare him to let a crab pinch his finger. But today, an unpredictable game actually sounded *fun*.

Even Jules perked up a little. "I do like a good dare."

Nia jumped up and down. "Yes, Truth or Dare! I want to go first!"

"Okay," Davy said immediately. "Truth or—"

"Dare!"

Davy crossed his arms and looked around. Then his eyes lit up. "I dare you to run to the end of the endless pier!"

"No problem," Nia said.

The kids followed her to the beginning of the pier. She stretched one leg, then stretched the other. Then she took off running. Earl Grey trotted after her, but he only made it a few steps before he stopped, panting.

Quincy smiled at Earl Grey. Earl Grey shrugged.

They watched as Nia ran farther and farther down the pier, her long brown braid streaming behind her. Finally, she disappeared on the horizon.

"How will we know if she actually made it?" Davy asked.

"She'll make it," Jules said. "Nia can run forever."

The kids continued down the boardwalk toward the really old rides. There was the old Ferris wheel with creaky bucket seats, and the older carousel with faded, eyeless horses, and the oldest teacup ride probably in the whole world, with giant chips and cracks in all the teacups.

"It's Davy's turn!" Runa said. "Truth or Dare?"

Quincy knew his best friend very well—well enough to know he'd pick *dare*. But to his surprise, Davy blushed and said: "Truth."

Maybe everyone was in a different mood today?

Runa tapped her chin thoughtfully. "If you could have any pet you wanted, what would you have?"

"A dog," Davy said right away.

Quincy giggled, and Jules rolled her eyes. Everyone knew dogs were just mythical creatures. But Runa beamed. "Awesome! I'd want a dragon. But a dog would be cool, too."

Davy grinned. "A dragon would definitely be a cool pet."

"Now it's your turn," Quincy told Runa. "Truth or dare?"

"Truth!"

Jules snorted. "Do you *ever* tell the truth, Runa?"

"Sometimes I tell the truth," she replied, "and sometimes . . . I tell *extra* truth."

"Have you ever seen a mermaid?" Quincy asked.

"Yes," Runa said firmly. Then: "Well, not exactly. Sort of?"

"Suuuure," Jules said. "Your turn, Quincy! Truth or Propagan—uh, I mean Dare?"

Normally, Quincy would pick truth. And everyone knew Jules gave the most challenging dares. But to everyone's surprise—including Quincy's—he said:

"Dare!"

Davy's eyes bugged out. "Really? I thought for sure you'd pick truth."

"I guess I'm in a daring mood today," Quincy said.

He watched as Jules turned in a slow circle, hands on her hips. "Aha!" she exclaimed, pointing toward the old bumper car rink. "I dare you to drive one of those bumper cars."

"Okay!" Quincy said cheerfully.

His friends gathered outside the rink as Quincy chose a yellow car and climbed in. He spun the steering wheel a few times to warm up. Normally, he would press the pedal hesitantly, edging forward little by little. But not today.

Today, he was in a daring mood.

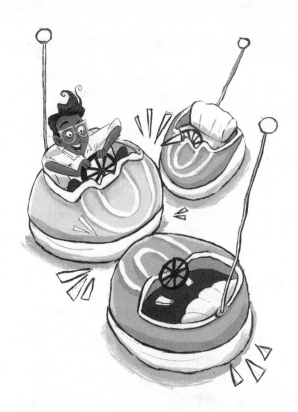

Quincy slammed his foot on the pedal, and his yellow car shot forward. "Wheee!" he exclaimed. His friends cheered. The little light at the top of his car's rod glowed, and Quincy felt like he was glowing, too.

He zoomed around and around the rink until he got dizzy. Then he changed directions and zoomed around and around the other way.

As he passed a pink car, its rod began to glow. Suddenly it shot toward Quincy—without a driver!

"Yikes!" He managed to swerve at the last second. The pink car bumped into the wall instead, then spun around and faced him.

"Quincy!" Jules called. "Look out!"

"Where?" Quincy looked around. All the other cars were still empty—but their rods had lit up. They started to move.

Straight toward Quincy!

He swerved left. He swerved right. Then he bumped into the orange car, and its light went out. His friends cheered again, and Quincy beamed.

He spun the steering wheel hard, stomped on the gas, and zoomed toward the pink car. *Bump!* Quincy sped away, and the blue car zipped toward him. Quincy drove faster, and so did the blue car. Then he saw a flash of purple, and—*bump!* The blue car skidded out of his way.

But Quincy hadn't bumped it—the purple car had. He stared in surprise.

"I think the purple car is trying to help you!" Jules called.

"Okay!" Quincy spun his car in a few fancy circles, then zoomed toward the green car. *Bump!* The purple car zoomed toward the orange car. *Bump!* Soon, Quincy's car and the purple car were the only ones left with lights on.

Slowly, he drove up to the purple car and peered at the driver's seat. Then he laughed. "It's my spirit!" he called to his friends.

"I think my spirit's in the orange car!" Runa exclaimed.

"And mine's in the blue car," Jules said. "I always wondered what our spirits do when it's not Spirit Day! I guess they haunt the old rides."

"Whew," Quincy said, climbing out of the yellow car. "At first I thought the cars were full of ghosts!"

"Which car was my spirit driving?" Davy asked. "I, um, couldn't tell."

"The red one," Quincy replied. "Yours was the first one I bumped."

"Oh." Davy looked relieved. Then he frowned. "Hey!"

After that, the kids headed back toward the beach. The ocean looked even more blue, and the sand looked even more sparkly, and the rock cats' smiles looked bigger than ever. Quincy smiled back at them.

SHLARPP!!!

He turned just as Runa tucked something inside her art supply bag. She wiped her sandy hand on her jeans.

"Hey! Was that another bottle?" Jules demanded.

"Nope." Runa's eyes sparkled like the ocean, and Quincy was glad she seemed happy again. "Just an extra-large saber tooth for a collage I'm—"

WONK! WONK! WONK!

All the kids swiveled around and stared at the lighthouse. A single pink light on top flashed with every *WONK* that blared. Quincy's smile flipped over and he clapped his hands over his ears.

"What does it mean?" Davy shouted over the *WONK*s.

Jules's eyes were as big and round as two cupcakes. "I have no idea, but I'd better take notes." She pulled out her notepad.

"Maybe it's a *new* warning?" Runa said. "My uncle's town has a new siren that goes off during the annual kite competition, so nobody will look up and think pterodactyls are attacking again—"

The lighthouse stopped *WONK*ing. Runa stopped talking.

Quincy smiled harder than ever. "Well, that was unpredictable," he said. "Shall we get back to Truth or Dare?"

Earl Grey nudged Jules's hand. "Snert? Snort?"

"Huh?" she said, glancing up from her notepad. "Oh, I'll skip my turn."

Suddenly Earl Grey let out a loud squeal and trotted down the beach as fast as he could.

"I didn't mean to hurt your feelings!" Jules called after him. "Sheesh. Watch hogs can be so sensitive."

"No, I think he sees something," Runa said. "Or someone."

Earl Grey seemed to be heading for the endless pier. Right where it vanished into the fog, Quincy saw a tiny speck. Soon the speck became a girl-shaped blob. Then the girl-shaped blob became a girl.

"It's Nia!" he exclaimed.

The kids reached the pier just as Nia jogged up. Earl Grey snorted and squealed happily. But Nia looked confused.

"What are you guys doing here?" she asked.

"What do you mean?" Jules said, pocketing her notepad. "We were right here at the beginning of the pier when you left!"

"This isn't the beginning of the pier," Nia argued. "It's the end!"

"No, it's the beginning!"

"It's the end!"

"Maybe the beginning *is* the end," Runa said. "Like the best stories."

Quincy gazed at the pier. Then he turned to his friends.

"Truth or Dare?"

"Dare," Jules said immediately.

"Dare," said Nia.

"Dare," said Davy.

"Dare," said Runa.

"Snort," snorted Earl Grey.

"I dare *everyone* to race to the beginning of the endless pier!" Quincy exclaimed.

Everyone grinned. Together, they raced down the pier, laughing all the way to the end.

Or the beginning.

Talise

Story 11:

It Takes a Village

Talise pressed her nose against her bedroom window. She could see a bit of ocean. For now, it looked perfectly normal.

But it wouldn't for long.

"An Extremely High Tide is definitely coming," she told the Town Committee for Lunar Consequences on the phone. "I've assessed every peculiar thing listed on the City Hall website, and I'm even more sure of it now."

"Yes, mm-hmm," the committee member replied. "I'll file your tip with the others. Thank you for—"

"Wait! Can you please tell my parents to unground me?"

The committee member paused. "Your parents? Wait a second—is this the kid who sent all those letters and e-mails?"

"Yes, that's me!" Talise said. "I know I've been quite persistent. But I can't work on my boat while grounded, and it's urgent that I finish before the . . . hello?"

The committee member had hung up.

Talise sighed. When Jules had published breaking news about the tide, Talise had thought her parents would unground her. But then the committee had called the news propaganda— and everyone had believed them.

Talise knew preparing for an Extremely High Tide was a lot of work.

So was evacuating the town.

But so was building a boat. At this point, Talise could never finish it in time. If she ever saw her boat again, it'd be a partially finished boatwreck on the ocean floor. If her parents ever allowed her to dive again, that is.

She squeezed her sea blob. A tear fell onto it.

There was a knock on her bedroom door. Talise opened it, then went and sat on her bed. Her parents came in and sat on either side of her. They appeared Loving/Concerned, as usual.

"You have a visitor," her mother said.

Talise felt mystified. "Is it the committee? Did they change their minds?" Then she narrowed her eyes. "It's not another rubber duck, is it?"

"Fortunately not!" Clara smiled at Talise from the doorway.

Talise didn't smile back. She liked Clara a lot, but she didn't feel happy enough on the inside for it to show on the outside. "Hello," she said. "How was Puerto Rico?"

"Lovely," Clara replied, sitting in Talise's desk chair. "Your parents tell me you've been grounded. Do you want to tell me why?"

"She's not supposed to—" Talise's father began.

"Sorry, but I'd like to hear from Talise," Clara interrupted.

Talise felt surprised. Her parents had never let her fully explain. "I'm not supposed to dive in the *deep*-deep sea without a buddy," she began. "So I found one! Her name is Runa, and she has black hair cut into angles. She's also an artist, but I trusted her because I thought she trusted me underwater. But seventy-four minutes was too long to wait. Now I realize I shouldn't have trusted her in the first place, because she tells a lot of stories, and stories are just another kind of lie."

"I see," Clara said.

"You do?" Talise's parents said.

"I'm getting better at understanding Talise's dialect." Clara winked at Talise, then turned back to her parents. "But I think there was a misunderstanding between the three of you. Did you specify that Talise's dive buddy needed to dive *underwater* with her?"

Talise's mother glanced at Talise's father. "Did we?"

"I thought we did," he replied. "Now I'm not sure."

"See?" Talise said. "I didn't break any rules."

"Not technically," Clara agreed. "Then again—when your parents told you not to dive in the *deep*-deep sea without a buddy, did you understand what they actually meant? Even if they didn't specify it?"

"NO, I—" Talise paused. Then she sighed. "I suppose I did.

But my parents should trust me. As a bathymetrist, I know more about the ocean than any kid in Topsea—"

"And all the grown-ups, too!" her father said. "We know. And we are so proud of you."

"But even the most experienced scuba diver in the world can run into trouble sometimes," her mother said. "What if you got stuck? Or your fancy vest malfunctioned?"

"I am quite vigilant about BCD maintenance," Talise said.

Then she frowned.

"It's not that I don't *want* to dive with a buddy—even on shallow dives! But nobody expresses any interest in it. Not even you, Mom and Dad."

Then she sighed.

"Maybe I'd have a diving buddy if I had a best friend. I'm the only kid in Ms. Grimalkin's class without one. Usually, I don't mind—but sometimes I do. There's just nobody who shares my interests."

Then she sniffled.

"Or in the case of my boat, nobody who even believes me!"

Talise's parents and Clara glanced at each other. "I think you'd be surprised," Talise's mother said.

* * *

As they entered the living room, Runa bounced up from the couch. "I'm sorry I told on you, Talise," she said. "I really do trust you!"

"Thank you," Talise said. "I am no longer extremely upset."

"It's just, sometimes my imagination runs away with me," Runa said. "Believe it or not. While I was waiting for you on the pier, I imagined a sea serpent coiled around your BCD and air tank, squeezing until it burst and you had nothing in your regulator except seawater, and meanwhile seaweed stole your weight belt, and nitrogen bubbles formed in your joints. . . ."

Talise's parents stared at Runa in horror. But Talise grinned. "You've been reading the dive book?"

"I have! And I started *The Great Book of Boatbuilding*, but I didn't get to finish before Jules wanted it back."

"Jules was reading *The Great Book of Boatbuilding*?" Talise said. "But she's never any expressed interest in boatbuilding! Nobody has."

Runa and Clara and Talise's parents glanced at each other. "I think you'd be surprised," Runa said.

* * *

Talise walked to the beach with her parents, Clara, and Runa. The air was approximately 74 degrees Fahrenheit, while the ocean was closer to 62 degrees. She could see the sun and moon at the same time.

Visiting the beach always made Talise feel thrilled on the inside, even if she usually knew what to expect. She definitely didn't expect Quincy and Davy and Nia and Jules and Finn and Earl Grey!

"We're all here to help you finish your boat!" Nia exclaimed, clapping her hands.

"My boat?" Talise felt disbelief. "But why?"

"Because it's important to you," Runa said.

"Because we trust you," Quincy added.

"Because you know more about the ocean than anyone in Topsea," Jules said. "*Especially* the Town Committee for Lunar Consequences and Totally Slanderous Accusations."

"And also, because of this." Runa signaled to Earl Grey, who trotted over. Talise noticed he had something in his mouth.

SHLORPP!!!

Runa tugged the bottle from Earl Grey's mouth, then handed it to Talise. "I found it the other day on the beach! I kept it a secret, like our other one."

"I *knew* that wasn't a saber tooth," Jules said.

Speechless, Talise examined the bottle. It looked even older than all the others. She pulled out the cork and shook out a rolled-up piece of tree bark.

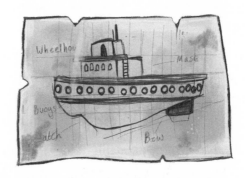

"Definitely a boat," Clara said.

Talise nodded adamantly. "Indeed. I am thrilled you finally see it! Each message seems to be a schematic for a different type of boat. The first one was a motorboat. The second one was a sailboat. This one appears to be a tugboat, because it has a wheelhouse and a mast and—"

"Also, there's a drawing of a tugboat," Runa said, pointing.

"Ah, yes," Talise said. "That is also helpful."

"I'm sorry I ever doubted you," Jules said. "I should've trusted your hunch—especially since you trusted mine."

"Where should we start?" Talise's father saluted her. "You're the captain!"

Talise couldn't believe her eyes. But then they filled with tears. So did her parents' eyes. Also Earl Grey's eyes. Even Clara sniffled a bit.

"I am very grateful," Talise said. "Building a boat alone is hard work. With eleven assistants, it might be finished a little sooner. Possibly even before arrival of the Extremely High Tide."

Quincy gulped. "I hoped everything would be okay."

"It *will* be okay!" Nia patted his curly head. "It always is. As long as we batten all the hatches in time."

"Okay," Talise said. "First, everyone grab a plank from that big pile of wood."

"What pile?" Runa asked.

Talise turned around. Her boatbuilding supplies were where she had left them—but where her giant pile of wood had sat, there was only a giant, woodpile-shaped dent in the sand. Only a few twigs were left—along with a sign on a thick piece of paper:

BOATS ARE DANGEROUS

and should be avoided

"Someone must have taken it!" Talise said. She knew her anxiety was showing on the outside. "We can't finish the boat without any wood!"

"Where can we get a lot of wood quickly?" Davy asked.

"I have a friend who lives in the beach forest!" Finn exclaimed. Then he glanced at Runa, his dialect switching from Friendly to Mouse. "Um, a new friend."

"Your friend lives in the forest?" Runa gasped. "That explains your aura! Why didn't you just tell me about them?"

"I should have. It's just . . ." Finn shuffled his feet. "He's a little unusual."

Runa laughed. "Finn! If you like him, I'll like him. I just missed you, that's all."

"I missed you too."

They hugged. "On the bright side," Runa said, "it gave me the chance to get to know Talise better, too. Just wait till I tell you about all our adventures . . ."

Talise shook her head. But she couldn't help smiling. Whatever Runa's dialect was (Baffling/Amusing?), Talise was starting to enjoy it.

While the other kids combed the beach for more driftwood, Finn led Clara and Talise's parents to the beach forest. In record time, they returned in Clara's truck piled with logs. A boy stood atop them. He had disheveled white-blond hair and wore a crown of sticks and leaves, just like Finn's. His eyes were two different colors, Talise noticed. That was quite unusual.

Finn introduced the feral child to his friends. "Thank you for your help," he said. "Don't feel obligated to stick around, but . . ."

148

"I'm right where I'm supposed to be," the feral child said. "In fact, I've read quite a few library books about boatbuilding. Do you have an adze? Or maybe an awl and gimlets?"

"In every size," Talise replied.

As a bathymetrist, Talise had already known more about the ocean than anyone in Topsea. Now she knew more about boats than anyone in Topsea, too. And with so much help, the boat came together in no time.

Best of all, everyone brought their own talents to the table.

Runa showed Jules how to draw diagrams in the sand. "Now that my vision has cleared, I've been getting into technical drawing."

Davy organized an assembly line to speed up the process. "My mom is an assembly line manager at the seaweed cracker factory," he explained.

Nia and Earl Grey took charge of the heavy lifting, although they paused every few minutes to jump for joy. Quincy ran back and forth from his house with as many baked goods as he could carry.

Clara and Talise's parents took charge of the sawing, and everybody hammered until their arms were sore. The feral child climbed the mast and secured the sail.

Runa stood back. "Needs more bells and whistles and glitter and whirligigs," she said.

"We have glitter, at least!" Davy grabbed Runa's spray glitter and sprayed until the whole boat shimmered. "Oops, that's kind of a lot."

Talise shrugged. "Maybe it'll help with waterproofing?"

Finn removed his crown of sticks and leaves, then placed it on the ship's rudder. The feral child removed his crown of sticks and leaves, then placed it on Finn's head. "I can always make another," he said.

There was only one thing left to do.

"Every boat needs a name," Clara said. "What do you want to call it, Talise?"

"Me?" Talise said.

"Of course!" Runa handed her a paintbrush. "It's your boat."

"I suppose that's logical." Talise stood back, gazing at the boat. *Her* boat. A boat's name should be comforting, she thought.

She stepped forward and painted its name on the side.

S.S. SEA BLOB

When she finished, everybody was thrilled on the outside. "What a great boat!" Davy grinned. His teeth glittered.

"Probably the best boat in the entire world!" Nia said.

"Factually the best," Jules corrected her.

"One question," the feral child said. "I kept meaning to ask, but: What kind of boat is it supposed to be, exactly?"

Talise scratched her head. "Well . . . it's not just one kind of boat. Since all the schematics were from different kinds of boats, I decided to combine them. So it's a motorboat. And also a sailboat. And also a tugboat."

"Probably the best motor-sail-tugboat in the entire world!" Nia said.

"Factually the best," Jules corrected her.

"But what is it supposed to tug?" asked the feral child.

"It's . . ." Talise began.

Everyone waited. She knew they were staring at her, but she kept staring at her boat. She squeezed her sea blob.

She'd avoided thinking about the *reason* for building her boat. All she'd ever known was that she *had* to. It was one of the strongest inside-feelings she'd ever had. A hunch, Jules had called it. But now that the boat was finished . . .

"I guess building a boat *was* pretty silly," Talise said.

"No way," Runa reassured her. "It was actually super fun!"

"Like howling at the moon," Finn joked.

"And anyway, that's the thing about hunches," Jules said. "There's always a reason for them—sometimes, you just don't know it right away."

Clara nodded in agreement. "You just have to trust yourself."

Talise thought about it. She couldn't expect her classmates and parents and Clara and the feral child to trust her if she didn't trust herself.

And she did! She *did* trust herself.

"While I have you all here," Talise began, "would you mind accompanying me to City Hall? My boat is safe from the Extremely High Tide. But we should probably make sure the rest of Topsea is safe, too."

Jules sighed. "You think they'll finally listen?"

"If we're all together, they have to!" Runa slung an arm around Jules's neck. "Talise, we're right behind you."

TALISE'S LOGBOOK

Name: Talise Villepreux

Date: Monday

Location: Topsea beach, City Hall

Time in: N/A **Time out:** N/A **Bottom Time:** N/A

Depth: Out of my*

Temperature: Ominous

Visibility: A little misty, but that could just be my eyes

Observations: The good news is that my boat is finished. Thanks to my family and classmates and the boy from the beach forest, the S.S. *Sea Blob* is ready to sail!

The bad news is an Extremely High Tide is coming.

An Extremely High Tide is only dangerous if the town does not prepare in time. But when my friends and I asked the Town Committee for Lunar Consequences to send out a notification just in case, they said, "We can't stake the committee's reputation on a random kid's prediction" and "Paper doesn't grow on trees" and "Please stop talking, I haven't had enough coffee to deal with this."

* I think that was a good joke!

Finally, the committee agreed to take another look at their charts. Even though they appeared to be games of tic-tac-toe, I am feeling quite optimistic.

Perhaps it is because I know my parents trust me. Clara trusts me. Runa, Jules, Finn, Davy, Nia, and Earl Grey trust me. Quincy trusts me (even though he is quite apprehensive and would prefer to trust the committee). You trust me, Logbook. I trust me, too.

Or perhaps it is because I trust the ocean.

Story 12:

The Why Silo

D avy didn't care for seaweed.

Not that he would ever say that out loud—especially on Bring Your Kid to Work Day. His mom worked at the seaweed cracker factory, and he didn't want to hurt her feelings. (Also a stray, spying strand might overhear him.)

Everyone else in Topsea *loved* seaweed. Davy didn't get it! Sometimes he thought if he learned *why* his friends went bananas over seaweed pops and seaweed snow cones, he'd understand Topsea better, too.

Fake it till you make it had worked on Spirit Day. So Davy decided he'd pretend to like seaweed until he really did like it.

He pretended really, really hard. Maybe a little too hard.

"Where'd you get all that stuff?" his mom asked at breakfast.

Davy looked down at his *Eat Local Seaweed!* T-shirt, woven seaweed belt, skinny seaweed shoelaces, and *Seaweed Rocks* flag. "Principal King loaned it to me from the lost and found. Although I think the flag is hers."

"That's very sweet, Davy. I'm glad you're so excited to see the factory!"

He smiled, although he couldn't help feeling a little envious of his friends. Quincy was going to his mom's horticulture lab to learn about plant physiology and flower psychology. Nia was flying to Playa del Carmen to look at beachfront mansions. Runa was going to the moon. Or her father's cheese shop. Davy wasn't sure which, but both sounded fun and interesting.

Maybe going to the seaweed cracker factory would be fun and interesting, too.

Davy's mom usually took the triple-decker bus to work. Because the weather was especially nice, they sat on the top level. By the time they reached the factory, their hair stuck up in all directions and they couldn't stop laughing.

"This is why I always carry a beachcomb on sunny days," Davy's mom said.

As she fixed Davy's hair, he noticed a few workers in bright yellow vests. They were lining up orange cones leading to the bluffs. "Do you think they're preparing for the Extremely High Tide?" he asked.

"Last I heard, the Town Committee for Lunar Consequences was still running tests," his mom replied. "But it sure looks like it, doesn't it?"

"They'd better be! Talise is more of an expert than that committee."

Davy's mom chuckled. "You seem pretty excited."

It was true. Davy *really* wanted to experience an Extremely High Tide! (Although he'd never admit that to Quincy.)

They approached the bluffs. One side looked like a row of towering chimneys made of moss-covered granite, all different heights and widths. Davy had never seen the seaweed cracker factory up close. Now he could see a little door at the bottom, and little windows peeking out from behind the moss, and little plumes of smoke puffing out of the tops of the "chimneys."

Maybe today was going to be fun and interesting after all!

Davy's mom showed a security guard her ID, which she wore on a seaweed lanyard. The guard gave Davy a visitor sticker. He stuck it to his *Eat Local Seaweed!* T-shirt.

"Nice shirt!" the guard said. "Bet you'd like some seaweed gum."

"Um, sure," Davy said.

He slipped the stick of gum into his pocket instead of his mouth. Once again, he couldn't help but wonder *why*. Why would anyone want seaweed gum, when they could have spearmint or watermelon or grape?

Davy followed his mom inside. Their footsteps echoed around the stone walls as they walked down a long corridor. Davy didn't see anyone else, but he thought he heard the faint murmur of voices.

And ticking. And grating. And pulverizing.

They stepped into an elevator. As they rode up, Davy's mom fitted a hairnet around his head, pulling the elastic down to cover all of his shaggy brown hair.

"I think you'll like this part."

"Wearing a hairnet?" Davy said uncertainly.

His mom laughed, putting on her own hairnet. "No, seeing the factory floor."

Davy waited eagerly as the elevator went up . . . and up . . . and *up*. They must have been almost to the top of the bluffs when it finally stopped. The doors slid open. Davy stepped out onto a metal platform and looked down.

"Wow!" he exclaimed.

The massive factory floor spread out far below him, a dizzying series of conveyor belts covered in piles of squiggling seaweed and sparkling salt and colorful powders. Robotic arms with rubber grippers lifted boxes. Printing presses spit out labels for various cracker flavors. Super-tall silos huffed and puffed and occasionally grunted things like "Ugh, Mondays" or "Get back to work, Bob."

Hundreds of workers milled around, all wearing hairnets and bright green one-piece rubber suits. Some carried clipboards, which they marked after examining a finished cracker. Others carried tiny spoons, for sampling the piles of flavored powder. A

few wore thick gloves, for wrangling particularly unruly strands of seaweed into the dehydrator.

"Right this way!" Davy's mom said.

Davy followed her down the platform, his eyes still glued to the factory floor. If he was going to figure out why everyone in Topsea loved seaweed so much, this definitely looked like the place to do it.

But when they reached a door labeled *Taste Test Room*, Davy's smile grew forced. He really didn't want to taste any seaweed crackers. Still, he waved his *Seaweed Rocks* flag dutifully as he walked inside.

More workers in rubber suits sat behind a large, circular table covered in little plates. Each plate had a stack of crackers in various colors: green, orange, yellow-green, orange-yellow, greener-green, black.

"Sorry for interrupting," Davy's mom said. "Luis, this is my son, Davy. Davy, this is Luis, the Experimental Flavors Manager."

The man closest to Davy stood up. He had curly black hair and a curlier black mustache dusted with cracker crumbs.

"Welcome, Davy!" he said. "Would you like to try a few new flavors we're working on? We'd love to get a kid's opinion."

Davy did his best to sound enthusiastic. "Sure, thanks!"

He walked around the table to an empty chair and sat. Luis passed him a piece of paper, a pencil, and several little plates of crackers. Each was labeled with a different flavor:

Pickled Pumpkin

Hickory-Smoked Eggplant

Caramel Clam

Spicy Duck l'Homage

"What we're doing is tasting each cracker," Luis explained. "Then taking notes on the pros and cons of the flavors. Don't be afraid to write the cons," he added with a wink. "If you don't like the taste, it would really help us to know why."

Why? Davy thought. *Because it tastes like seaweed, that's why!*

But he just said, "Okay!"

"Jalapeño Honey!" Davy's mom snatched a cracker, then bit into it with a loud crunch. "This one's fantastic, Luis."

Davy took one, too, but he just nibbled off the corner. To his surprise, it wasn't that bad. He picked up his pencil and paused, thinking. The reason he liked it was because the spiciness of the jalapeño and the sweetness of the honey covered up the seaweediness of the seaweed. But he wasn't sure Luis would appreciate that kind of feedback. So instead, he wrote:

Pros: *Spicy, sweet.*
Cons: *None.*

Next, he tried the Pickled Pumpkin.

Pros: *Halloweeny.*
Cons: *Puckery.*

Then he tried the Caramel Clam.

Pros: *Caramelly.*

Cons: *Clammy.*

Davy was starting to enjoy himself. Being a taste tester wouldn't be such a bad job, he thought. Even at a seaweed cracker factory.

But then he got to the last plate, piled with black crackers. The label read:

"Crab"

Davy eyed the crackers suspiciously.

Then the door opened. A petite woman with spiky brown hair stepped inside. When she saw Davy's mom, she heaved a sigh of relief.

"There you are!" she exclaimed. "We're holding an emergency meeting in five minutes. Our drainage system is backed up, and we need to come up with a plan to fix it fast, just in case there's an Extremely . . . uh, extremely unexpected event."

"Right behind you," Davy's mom said, then turned to Davy. "Do you want to hang out in the taste test room until I'm done?"

"That's okay, I'm pretty full," he replied quickly. "Can I watch the assembly lines instead?"

"As long as you're careful," she said, kissing his hairnet.

Luis waved. "Thanks for the feedback!"

Back on the metal platform, Davy walked to the railing and leaned over as far as he dared, watching the activity below.

He found the silos especially interesting. They looked like giant metal coffee cans, so tall they almost reached the platform.

Each had a hatch on top, and a square-shaped door with a dial lock, like a locker. And each had a different word painted in green along the side:

CRUNCH

TANG

AROMA

BITTER

SWEET

WHY

Davy furrowed his brow. "Why" wasn't a taste word. But it was a question he'd been asking all day: *Why did everyone in Topsea love seaweed so much?*

Maybe the answer was in that silo!

Whistling innocently, Davy strolled down the platform until he stood over the WHY silo. He glanced at the workers, but they were all too busy to look up.

Carefully, he slipped under the railing and dropped onto the silo with a light thunk. He crawled over to the hatch and studied the dial. Unlike his locker at school, this lock's combination used letters instead of numbers.

Not far from the dial, someone had scratched the word "AROO."

Davy laughed. His dad used to have trouble remembering passwords. He'd scrawl hints for himself on the back of his phone or under his computer. When his mom saw one, she'd sigh and cross her arms and pretend to be mad. "It's too risky!" she would say. "What if someone guesses the password?"

"No way," Davy's dad would reply. "No one can guess *my* hints."

Was AROO a hint? Davy chewed his lip. Then he twisted the dial to *D*, then to *O*, then to *G*.

CLICK.

Davy grinned. He wondered what his dad would have said—probably that *his* hint would have been a lot harder to guess.

He pulled open the hatch. A bat swooped out.

"Yikes!" Davy ducked.

Once the bat was out of sight, he peered into the darkness and spotted a ladder. He shimmied through the opening, grabbed the top rung, and lowered himself inside.

His footsteps echoed off the walls as he descended. When he reached the fifth rung, there was a *SPLOOSH!*

Davy glanced down in surprise. His right foot was underwater. Grimacing, he pulled his foot out and steadied himself. His eyes were starting to adjust now. Leaning out as far as he dared, he stared into the water. It reminded him of the Bottomless Cove.

"Hmm," he said.

Suddenly the water shimmered, then rippled, then began to churn. It moved faster and faster, like a whirlpool.

Davy couldn't take his eyes off it. He'd gone to a carnival once, and a hypnotist had tried to put him into a trance with a whirling black-and-white circle. *It didn't work at all*, he thought dizzily. *She tried to make me cluck like a chicken when she rang a bell, but I just laughed. . . .*

He stretched out even farther, farther, until his nose grazed the surface, and the water moved faster and faster until—

"*Davy?*"

It sounded like Davy's mom. Startled, he jerked away from the water. Hadn't it been whirling? It was so still now.

How long had he been staring?

He scrambled up the ladder and out of the hatch, closing it quietly behind him. Then he pulled himself onto the platform, stuck his hands in his pockets, and casually strolled toward the Emergency Meeting Room.

"There you are!" Davy's mom said. "Meeting's all finished. Would you like to try working behind one of the assembly lines? Or maybe try wrangling seaweed into the hydrator?"

Davy opened his mouth to say yes. But the moment his mom said "seaweed," his mouth started watering.

"Can we go back to the Taste Test Room?" he heard himself ask. "I really want to try more of those experimental flavors."

His mom raised her eyebrows. "Really?"

"And tonight, could we have seaweed burgers for dinner? Or seaweed loaf? Or Quincy makes seaweed pancakes sometimes— maybe we can try that?"

"Of course," his mom said, still watching him curiously. "But,

Davy, I know you don't really like seaweed that much. You don't have to pretend just for me."

Davy glanced back at the silo and grinned. "That's because I didn't understand *why* everyone in Topsea loves seaweed so much. But I get it now. It's . . . it's *seaweed*."

HWAA! HWAA! HWAA!

They looked up as green lights began flashing in the corridor.

"What's going on?" Davy asked. "Is that an alarm for Extremely High Tide?"

"No, that alarm is much louder," his mom said. "This alarm just warns that another alarm might be sounding soon. Nothing to be concerned about. Shall we do a little more taste testing?"

"Sure!"

"But first—why is your shoe soaking wet?"

"I stepped in a seaweed," Davy said distractedly. "I mean, a puddle." He was busy imagining all the new, delicious dishes he could try. Seaweed steak, seaweed pizza, seaweed doughnuts . . .

NOTIFICATION: SAFETY PROTOCOL FOR EXTREMELY HIGH TIDES

From the Town Committee for Lunar Consequences and Look Out!

Apologies, everyone. After being inundated by tips from armchair scientists (including a dozen in person—please wear shoes when visiting City Hall, thank you), we decided to take a second look at our findings. It turns out, an Extremely High Tide IS in fact on its way! Uh-oh! Don't worry—as long as safety protocol is followed, this "extreme" aquatic event can be survived in safety and style.

TWO HOURS BEFORE TIDE

- Batten all the hatches
- Hutch all the bats (and other small pets)
- Secure all nonamphibious large pets, or ensure they have access to flotation devices
- Store all electronics and other hydrophobic items in attics, upper shelving units, or basements below seafloor level
- Dress in waterproof clothing
- Stop by the Lost Soles shoe store, where Miss Meiko is celebrating the Extremely High Tide with a buy-one,

get-one-half-off sale on all galoshes! Just enter promo code SHLORPP!!! at checkout

ONE HOUR BEFORE TIDE

- Proceed in an orderly fashion to higher ground. This includes the bluffs, the seaweed cracker factory, and other prominent rooftops
- (The roof of the elementary school should probably be avoided)

TEN MINUTES BEFORE TIDE

- Wait for the alarm to sound
- STAND BACK, PLEASE

TIDE

- Enjoy!

FIFTEEN MINUTES AFTER TIDE

- Is the sea level back to normal (mostly)?
- Is the sun out (partially)?
- Then it is safe to return to your homes, schools, and work-places (probably)
- Don't say we didn't warn you!

Note on Beached Wildlife:

Before assisting any beached sea creature, make sure it is really in distress. The tide makes some animals quite happy. Like clams, for example. They love it.

THE TOPSEA SCHOOL GAZETTE

Today's Tide: EXTREMELY HIGH!!! (extremely soon)

WORD OF THE DAY:

Propaganda (n): A collection of information that may include selected facts, opinions, or wild embellishments that are presented as truth. This includes notifications issued by committees that make slanderous accusations against responsible reporters just because they're embarrassed that kids uncovered the truth while they were playing tic-tac-toe.

CALL AND . . . RESPONSE?

by Jules, Fifth-Grade Star Reporter

Extremely High Tide is the big news of the day, but there have been developments in the lighthouse keeper investigation, too. In addition to the flashing lights, the lighthouse has been sounding a wonky new warning, as if honking at something way, way out in the ocean. And this morning, this reporter heard a response!

A trumpetlike sound seems to be having a conversation with the lighthouse. Distant at first, it's getting closer by the minute. Is it a boat? Is it a ship? Where did it get a brass instrument, and why can't it carry a tune? This reporter might not have cracked this case yet, but one thing's for sure—we'll find out soon enough.

THE POETRY CORNER

Sweet as sugar

Nice as pie

Open as a book

Real as the sky

To fall in love

—Nia and Earl Grey

Story 13:

The Extremely High Tide

Talise

"Where do you think you're going?" Talise's father called.

"Drat," Talise muttered.

Slowly, she turned. Her mother and father stood in the entryway with their hands on their hips. They both wore galoshes. "Well?" her mother said.

Talise was no good at lying. "I was going to check on my boat," she admitted.

"But we leave for the bluffs in ten minutes!"

"And anyway, you checked twice this morning, honey," Talise's father added. "Also three times yesterday."

"Five times, in fact," Talise said worriedly. "I'm just

concerned about the anchor. Naturally, I triple-calibrated my sounding line before I measured the projected tidal depth, but I forgot to allow for feline interference—"

"For *what*?"

"The chance a rock cat might have chewed on its ending. I know it's unlikely. But if the boat isn't securely anchored, all my hard work will be swept out to sea."

"You have nothing to worry about," her mom reassured her.

"How do you know?" Talise squeezed her sea blob so hard it squeaked.

"Because nobody works harder than you," her father said, handing her a pair of galoshes decorated with purple starfish. "That's why we don't want *you* to be swept out to sea!"

Her mother nodded.

"Okay," Talise said with a sigh. She wouldn't mind being swept out to sea, but she knew better than to say it. "Just one request. Although I'm fond of these galoshes . . . could I please wear my flippers instead?"

Runa

Runa and Lina grinned at each other. They *loved* Extremely High Tides.

"Are all the hatches battened?" their mom asked, zipping up her raincoat.

"I've never been exactly sure what that means," their dad said, stuffing fancy cheeses into a cooler. "But the doors, windows, and basements are sealed."

"My important paintings are on the highest shelves," Runa said.

"My important paintings are on top of Runa's," Lina said.

"Looks like we're ready to—" their mom began, then sighed. "Isn't that enough cheese, dear?"

Runa giggled at her dad, who was having trouble closing the cooler. "Yeah, Dad," she said. "Extremely High Tides only last about fifteen minutes. Well, except for that one time, when it only lasted fourteen. . . ."

"Cheese is for *sharing*," he said loftily.

"I'm sure our fellow evacuees will welcome a wedge of Havarti or pepper jack," their mom said. "But now it's time to go!"

Principal King

Principal King fastened a waterproof poncho over her waterproof poncho. She glanced at her flag collection, then shook her head.

"I am not a fan of Extremely High Tides," she said.

Jules

"I still can't believe this is your first Extremely High Tide!" Jules said to Hazel as they climbed into the family van.

"I was out of town during all the others," Hazel replied, biting her nails.

"I guess our parents haven't been married *that* long. But what about last December? When the ocean left behind all those sea-salt icicles?"

"I slept through the whole thing, remember?"

"Oh, that's right." Jules giggled. "You do sleep like a chunk of driftwood."

"It's not funny!" Hazel wailed. "Okay . . . maybe it is. But I'm an investigative reporter, not a breaking newscaster covering natural disasters. I've memorized all the safety protocols from the Town Committee for Lunar Consequences and Look Out!—and I'm still nervous."

"You have nothing to worry about," Jules reassured her.

"How do you know?"

Jules didn't know for sure. But for the first time ever, she felt like her big sister's big sister. "Stick with me, and you'll be just fine," she said. "As long as your notepad is waterproof!"

Finn

Finn sat in the backseat beside his third-oldest brother. His first-oldest and second-oldest brothers rode in the middle seat. His dad sat in the passenger's seat, and his mom drove. They all wore shoes, even Finn.

Like most things in Topsea, the bluffs were only a few minutes away. But the line of cars winding uphill made the drive take longer, especially when they got stuck behind a triple-decker bus packed with evacuees.

"Are we there yet?" Finn's third-oldest brother complained.

"Put the pedal to the metal!" Finn's first-oldest brother said. "That's what I'd do if I was behind the wheel."

"No wonder you failed your driving exam," Finn said.

His parents and other brothers laughed.

Finally, they reached the top of the bluffs. A police officer waved them into a parking spot on the roof of the seaweed factory. Almost every car in town was there. Except for waterproof cars—people left those in their driveways.

"Your best friend's here," Finn's third-oldest brother said.

"Runa isn't my—" Finn began automatically. "Oh. Right."

For some reason, he still felt a little nervous seeing Runa. Even though she'd acted very understanding about his new friend, Finn knew he should have told her earlier. But as soon as he stepped out of the car, Runa tackled him with a big hug.

"So glad you made it! I've been keeping an eye out for your forest buddy, but I haven't seen him anywhere."

"I'm sure he's made his own arrangements in the beach forest," Finn said. "With his parents."

"His *wolf* parents?" Runa exclaimed.

"That's just a myth! Anyway, he'll be fine. He's very capable."

"I'm sure he is! But . . . well, my great-aunt told me that once during an Extremely High Tide, a kid hadn't evacuated by the time the alarm sounded, and they found him at the very top of the tallest tree in the entire forest—"

"I thought your great-aunt lived in South Korea," Finn said.

Runa paused. "Um . . . She does, but their high tides are even more extreme. Oh, look, there's Nia!" She waved her arms.

Nia bounced over to join them, then continued bouncing in place. She wore a white dress embroidered with colorful birds and flowers.

"I like your dress, Nia," Finn said.

"Thanks! I got it in Mexico City." Nia twirled. "Did you guys hear about Earl Grey? City officials gave him an official position as secondary alarm!"

"Wow!" Runa exclaimed. "You must be so proud. Where is he?"

"I'm not sure," Nia said. "I came early with Mama and Papa because Mama wanted valet. But I'm sure he'll do a great job."

"He's very clever," Finn agreed.

The Feral Child

The feral child applied one last strip of six-inch bidirectional filament tape to his tree yurt, then stood back. "Looks pretty secure, don't you think?"

His parents yipped.

Nia

Nia was so proud of Earl Grey, her heart was exploding!

She wanted to see him in action. But when she stopped by City Hall's information shelter, the committee member shook his head.

"Your watch hog didn't show up for work today," he said.

"What?" Nia screeched.

"Your watch hog didn't show up for—"

Nia sprinted away. She was so worried about Earl Grey her heart was breaking!

Nanny and Cosmo

"Nanny! Have you seen—" Nia skidded to a stop. "That's not Earl Grey."

"No, that's Cosmo," Nanny said.

Cosmo nodded in agreement.

"Um, hi, Cosmo," Nia said. "Have you seen Earl Grey? He never showed up for his secondary alarm job!"

"He didn't?" Nanny looked concerned. "*¡Qué lástima!* He was so excited about that gig, he snorted oatmeal all over our Oaxacan rug."

"What are we going to do? Extremely High Tide is on its way! I'm so worried about Earl Grey my heart is breaking. . . ." Suddenly Nia started giggling. "What were you two up to, anyway? Were you *smooching?*"

Cosmo's ears turned pink.

"We—" Nanny began.

"Never mind. I don't want to know!"

Ms. Grimalkin

Ms. Grimalkin pulled on a shower cap, careful not to puncture it with her long nails. She hated when her fur—er, hair—got wet. Then she squeezed through the hatch and stepped onto the roof of Topsea School.

"Everybody accounted for?" she asked her friends.

They purred.

Quincy

Quincy and Roxy frowned at each other. They *hated* Extremely High Tides.

By now, almost every person in Topsea was on top of the bluffs, the seaweed cracker factory, and other prominent rooftops. The most daring people crowded at the edge of the bluffs. Others sat in camp chairs, reading newspapers. Like it was just another day at the beach.

When it most certainly was not!

Quincy swallowed hard, then dropped one of the banana whoopie pies he was hugging. He'd stress-baked seven batches last night.

"Gwabbity," Roxy said anxiously, hiding her face in their mom's neck.

"That's right," she said, kissing the top of Roxy's curly head. "Gravity plays an important role in tides."

"I know you're anxious, but everything will be fine," Quincy told his sister, trying to sound brave and eager. "At least you have someone to hold you!"

His other mom winked. "We can hold you both if you want."

Yes, Mommy, please, I'm scared, thought Quincy. It came out, "That's okay, I'm fine," but she seemed to understand. She put an arm around Quincy's shoulders and kissed the top of his curly head, too.

"Oh, hey, isn't that your friend Davy?" she said.

"Yes, Mommy," Quincy began, then cleared his throat. "Oh.

Um . . . Er . . . Why *yes*, yes it is my friend Davy Jones. I will go stand beside him now."

Talise

WEEE! WEEE! WEEE!

"That's Earl Grey?" Davy exclaimed, his mouth full of whoopie pie. "Wow, he sounds just like an actual alarm."

Nia sighed gustily. "That's not Earl Grey."

"You sure?"

"Nia is right," Talise said. "That *is* an actual alarm—it means the Extremely High Tide is coming any minute now."

She stood with Runa, Finn, Jules, Quincy, Davy, and Nia at the edge of the bluffs. Not the *very* edge, but close. Runa, Finn, and Davy looked excited. Jules looked busy scribbling in her waterproof notepad. Quincy looked nervous. Nia looked worried. Talise wore flippers.

"Do all animals know what to do during an Extremely High Tide?" Nia asked Talise. "Naturally, I mean?"

"Marine creatures know to find lower ground," Talise replied with confidence. This was something she understood. "They burrow into the ocean floor or find passageways in the coral reefs, or in the case of the seal family I'm acquainted with, they secure their children with kelp leashes—"

Jules looked up from her notepad. "Earl Grey isn't a marine creature, though. He's a land creature."

"Land creatures I know less about," Talise said.

Nia wailed. "What's going to happen to him?"

"Animals take care of themselves," Finn said. "Even the rock cats. They always cram onto the roof of our school."

"And Earl Grey is an extremely capable pig," Talise said. She wasn't sure if that was a lie or the truth or a story, but it seemed to make Nia feel better. "In all likelihood, he is waiting out the tide somewhere safe."

"Or he's helping someone else," Runa said. "Like all good watch hogs do."

Earl Grey

WEEE! WEEE! WEEE!

That's not me, said Earl Grey. It came out, "Weee?" but his voice was scratchy, since he'd just woken up from a nap under the boardwalk. He'd had trouble sleeping last night, since he was so nervous about his official position as secondary—

WEEE! WEEE! WEEE!

Uh-oh.

Earl Grey glanced around. The lighthouse was flashing faster than ever. Was he too late? The beach was empty.

The ocean, however . . .

Davy

WHOOOSH!

"Here it comes!" Davy jumped up and down. "The Extremely High Tide! *Yahooooo*—oof!"

"Stop that," Quincy said. He'd thrown a whoopie pie at Davy.

Davy wiped whoopie pie from his eye socket. "I'm not the only one who's excited!" He pointed at Finn and Runa, who appeared to be dancing.

"*AROOOOO!*" Finn howled.

Davy felt like howling, too. He'd just never seen anything like it!

The ocean was no longer where it belonged. It was *everywhere*! On Main Street and Front Street and Back Street, and in the schoolyard and beach forest and covering the entire boardwalk. All kinds of peculiar things swirled into town: writhing tangles of seaweed, buoys, animate and inanimate sea blobs, a glowball, and dozens and dozens of copies of *Everything Else You Need to Know About Topsea*.

"This is so cool!" Davy said.

"If you say so," Quincy muttered.

"It is! It—" Davy glanced over his shoulder. "Are you backing up?"

"No," Quincy said, backing up.

Davy picked up one of the whoopie pies Quincy dropped. "These would be better with seaweed," he began, then paused. On a ledge partway down the bluffs, he noticed fishermen and women slinging nets into the rushing water. Whenever they hauled one out, they all checked it, then laughed. "What are they doing down there?"

"Competing for the weirdest catch!" Jules replied. She had her arm around Nia, who was less bouncy than usual, but not as anxious-looking as before.

"How does everything dry off, anyway?" Davy asked.

"The sun always comes out after an Extremely High Tide," Runa replied. "Hotter and brighter than ever. So hot and bright, in fact, that one time it evaporated the water so fast a thunderstorm began immediately—"

"Runa loves a good thunderstorm," Finn added.

"I do!" Runa beamed. "You never know what might fall out of the sky. Boots! Cats! Boots and cats! Dogs, even!"

"Cats and dogs together!" Finn joked.

Everybody giggled. Including Talise.

Talise

SHLORPP!!!

As the ocean began to recede, Talise walked back over to her parents and told them Finn's joke.

"It's funny because in the Legend of the Dogs, dogs and cats are mortal enemies," she explained. "As recounted in

Everything You Need to Know About Topsea, volume one. I still haven't read the second volume, but I ordered it a long time ago—"

"There's one!" her father exclaimed, pointing at a book drifting by.

"I *knew* I should have brought a net," Talise said.

Her mother smiled at her. "Luckily, you have a deep-sea-diving license."

"And a boat," her father said, tugging one of Talise's pigtails. "Oh, look, the sun is coming out!"

HWEEE! HWEEE! HWEEE!

Talise gasped. "That's definitely Earl Grey!"

Earl Grey

Earl Grey lowered his snout.

He had ridden out the entire tide from an extremely high perch: Talise's boat. Maybe it wasn't the official position for his official position, but he'd still completed his duties as secondary alarm.

As usual, the Extremely High Tide had strummed and stirred and swept all kinds of undersea things into town. Usually, the tide brought them back out again, but it always left some behind. Including a few sea creatures who hadn't swum to lower ground, or secured themselves with kelp leashes.

Like the sea creature beached on the beach down below.

Earl Grey leaped off the boat—*HWEE!*—then galloped over to help, teacup bouncing wildly.

It was a big lump of a creature. More blobby than a seal. More shapely than a sea blob. The long, fancy sort of tooth growing from its head looked an awful lot like a unicorn horn. It was a magical animal.

A narwhal.

Not a stuffed narwhal like Nia's friend Davy had won for Earl Grey at the arcade. But a real, live narwhal. A beached one.

A narwhal-in-distress.

Earl Grey fell in love instantly.

Story 14:

Beached!

Flip. Flip. Flip. Flip.

Talise ran toward the sound of Earl Grey's alarm as fast as she could. Which wasn't very fast, because of her flippers.

She passed lots of brand-new tide pools filled with fascinating marine creatures that had just washed in.

She passed shells and teeth in all sorts of shapes and sizes.

She passed little pockets of sand that bubbled and blorped, as if they'd just swallowed bottles with secret messages.

But Talise didn't stop to look at any of these things. She only had eyes for her boat, bobbing up and down right where she'd left it.

"The S.S. *Sea Blob*!" she cried.

Talise saw Nia sprinting toward her boat from the other direction. She only had eyes for her watch hog, standing not far from the boat.

"Earl Grey!" Nia cried.

She looked as overjoyed as Talise felt. Earl Grey must have used the S.S. *Sea Blob* to stay safe during Extremely High Tide! He was a very capable watch hog, indeed.

"*HWEE-HWEE!*" Earl Grey cried. He sounded overjoyed, too. He only had eyes for . . . for what?

Talise rounded the boat's stern, then skidded to a halt beside Nia and Earl Grey. She gasped.

"Wow."

Davy, Quincy, Runa, Jules, and Finn caught up seconds later, all out of breath and rubbing stitches in their sides.

"*Wow.*"

For a moment, nobody spoke. They just gazed in awe at the enormous creature washed up on the beach. It was black and white with gray spots and a long, straight tusk that gleamed in the sunlight. Its shiny black eye blinked and blinked.

"It's a narwhal," Talise said at last.

She'd seen numerous pictures of them. But she'd never seen one in real life. Not in the deep sea, or even the *deep*-deep sea. No, this narwhal must have come from an even deeper sea than that.

"A narwhal?" Davy's brow furrowed. "I always thought those were just mythical. Like dragons. Or, um, dogs."

"Me too," Jules admitted. "But factually, they must be real, because we're looking at one."

Runa sighed. "It's so pretty. Look at that giant tooth!"

"Isn't it a tusk?" Finn asked. "Or maybe a horn?"

Quincy grinned. "Like a sea unicorn!"

"Technically, it's a tusk *and* a tooth," Talise said. "An elongated tooth. Marine creatures always secure themselves or move to lower ground during Extremely High Tide. Why didn't this one?"

"What are you *doing*?" Nia asked Earl Grey.

The watch hog appeared to be nuzzling the narwhal's face. The narwhal shifted, as if it wanted to move closer . . . but it barely budged an inch. It made a sound that was somehow big and little at the same time, like a whimper from a whale-size kitten.

"This is all my fault!"

The kids all turned. A woman stood behind them. She looked tall and graceful. Her black hair was swept up into a bun, and she wore a long navy dress with two rows of brass buttons that started at the collar and went all the way to the hem just above her ankles. Her feet were bare.

Jules let out a little squeak. "You're the lighthouse keeper! Aren't you?"

The lighthouse keeper nodded. Talise noticed Jules's hands were shaking as she flipped open her notebook, dropped it, picked it up, flipped it open again.

"Why were on you vacation for so long?" Jules asked. "No, wait. What were all those warnings about? No, wait. What do you mean, this is all your fault?"

"It's a long story," the lighthouse keeper said, toying with a chain around her neck. "It started when I went for a swim. A rather *long* swim."

Talise glanced at Runa, who smiled knowingly.

"During my swim, I lost something very important. This narwhal promised to look for it, and return it to me. I hitched a ride with a clam boater—but on the trip back, I realized an Extremely High Tide was on its way. So I began flashing a warning—"

"For the *narwhal!*" Jules's pen flew over her notebook. "You knew it might get swept up in the Extremely High Tide. And the narwhal was responding!"

The lighthouse keeper nodded. "My sweet but stubborn friend here insisted on returning my ring despite the risk."

Jules stopped writing. "Sorry, did you say *ring*?"

The lighthouse keeper pointed to the narwhal's tusk. Talise saw a ring sparkling on the very tip. The gold band was wide and shiny, with two silver strands coiled around either side.

"Oh." Jules stared at the ring. "It's . . . oh." Her dialect had changed, Talise noticed. Instead of Smart/Overbearing, she appeared Shocked/Confused.

Gently, the lighthouse keeper pulled the ring off the narwhal's tusk. She hung it on the chain around her neck. Then she placed her hand on the narwhal's face, just below its eyes.

"I'm sorry this happened," she whispered. "I'll find a way to help you home."

Earl Grey snorted and moved closer to the narwhal.

"But I think Earl Grey is in *love*!" Nia said, clutching at her heart. She turned to Talise. "A narwhal is a mammal, right? So it breathes air. It just needs to stay wet, You have that deep soaking tub—maybe the narwhal could live with you!"

Talise looked at Earl Grey and the narwhal. They did make an attractive pair. Maybe they had complementary auras? That was probably a good joke, but Talise knew jokes were all about timing. Right now it was best to tell the truth.

"The narwhal is a marine creature, not a land creature," she told Nia quietly. "It can't survive here, even in a bathtub."

"Land is no place for marine creatures," the lighthouse keeper agreed. She glanced at the rocks, where hundreds of yellow eyes stared at the narwhal. They appeared hungry. "Our friend must return to the ocean."

Nia's shoulders slumped. "My heart is *shattering*. But I get it."

Earl Grey shook his head. He looked quite defiant. But then the narwhal whimpered again, and the watch hog's shoulders slumped, too.

"Snoooort-sighh," he snorted.

Talise understood. "Earl Grey also wants to help the narwhal get home," she translated. "Even if he feels like his heart is shattering as well."

"We'll all help," Davy said. Quincy, Runa, Jules, and Finn nodded. At last, Nia nodded, too.

"Unfortunately, there are complications," Talise said. "Narwhals can weigh over three thousand pounds. Even with nine of us pushing, we won't be anywhere near strong enough to move it."

The lighthouse keeper gazed at the narwhal. The wind whipped a few loose strands of hair around her face. "Even if we *could* push," she said, "we wouldn't be able to push the narwhal out to the *deep*-deep sea. But if we release it in shallow water, the tides would bring it right back to shore."

The narwhal sighed. It missed the ocean. Talise could translate easily, because she knew how it felt.

All of a sudden her heart started pounding hard against her ribs.

"What about a boat?" she asked.

Runa stared at Talise. So did the lighthouse keeper. So did Nia, Jules, Davy, Quincy, Finn, Earl Grey, and the narwhal. Everyone was staring at Talise.

But for once, she didn't mind.

"The S.S. *Sea Blob* is a motor-sail-tugboat," she explained, her voice trembling with excitement. "The sails catch the wind and help the boat move speedily. The motor gives the boat more power. And the tug is designed to move much larger vessels. . . ."

Talise took a deep breath.

"Theoretically, the S.S. *Sea Blob* is powerful enough to tug a beached narwhal back into the ocean!"

The lighthouse keeper looked from Talise to the S.S. *Sea Blob*, then back to Talise. "Is that *your* boat?"

Talise nodded. "I built it. *We* built it," she corrected herself. Her friends smiled.

"But mostly, it was Talise," Runa said. "She dove a hundred thousand miles under the sea and studied all kinds of boats, and she memorized twenty million books about boatbuilding, and now she knows more about boats than anyone in the *universe*."

"Is that true?" the lighthouse keeper asked Talise, her eyes wide.

Talise paused. A lot of what Runa just said wasn't true. But that didn't mean Runa was *lying*. She'd embellished the truth, but she meant every word. At long last, Talise knew Runa's dialect.

Runa was Imaginative/Sincere.

"It's the truth, plus a little *extra* truth," Talise said, and Runa grinned.

"Amazing!" the lighthouse keeper exclaimed. "What should we do to prepare the S.S. *Sea Blob*, Talise?"

Talise stood up straighter. "Runa, Finn, Davy, and Nia, secure the end of the main towline around the narwhal. Earl Grey, supervise and make sure the narwhal is comfortable. Jules, you read *A Great Book of Nautical Terms*—do you remember how to tie a slipped buntline knot?"

Jules flipped through her notebook. "Yes! I drew a how-to diagram."

"Use that knot to attach the other end of the main towline to the mooring hitch," Talise went on. "Miss Lighthouse Keeper—"

"Suvanna," the lighthouse keeper said. "My name is Suvanna."

"Suvanna, will you please come on board with me?" Talise asked. "I need someone to lift the anchor while I manage the wheelhouse."

"Of course," Suvanna replied.

Talise looked around at her friends. "Does everyone understand their tasks?"

"Aye-aye, Captain!" they said in chorus.

All the kids got to work. With so many hands, they finished their tasks in no time. Talise stood on the deck, the happiest she'd ever felt on dry land.

"Is everyone ready?" she called.

"Not everyone," Nia said, motioning to Earl Grey. His tail drooped, teacup dragging in the sand as he nuzzled the narwhal one last time.

"It's a terrible curse," Suvanna said sadly, "to be stuck on land when your heart lies with the sea."

Talise knew exactly what she meant. Then she had an idea.

"Earl Grey!" she called. "Maybe you can't live in the sea, but you can visit. I can take you out on the S.S. *Sea Blob* anytime you like. You could even get a diving license, if you don't mind a little bookwork."

"Squee-oink!" Earl Grey exclaimed. The narwhal made a similar sound, its dark eyes sparkling.

Nia clasped both her hands to her heart. "He said thank you so much, and you're his all-time favorite sea captain!"

Talise grinned. "Yes, I understood him as well."

She waved to her friends. Then she headed back to the wheelhouse. Once she was in position behind the steering station, she stuck her head out of the window. "Anchors aweigh!"

The lighthouse keeper heaved the rope, pulling the anchor out of the sand.

SCHLORRRP!!!

Talise pushed the throttle forward. The propellers began to whir—and with a ceremonial water salute that streamed high in the air, the S.S. *Sea Blob* started moving forward.

Back on shore, everybody cheered.

Talise tilted the lever that controlled the rudders, and the boat turned slightly. The whole entire great big ocean spread out in front of her as far as her eyes could see. Wow! She'd spent so much time *in* the ocean, she'd never realized how much fun it could be to spend time *on* the ocean.

It really floated her boat.

Talise smiled. That was definitely a good joke.

Once the S.S. *Sea Blob* was a good, long distance from shore, Talise pulled the throttle back. The boat slowed to a drift.

She joined Suvanna at the stern of the boat. "Jules did an excellent job with this knot," she said, patting the towline secured to the mooring hitch. Then she pulled it. The rope came undone, freeing the narwhal.

The narwhal gathered the rope around its tusk. It lifted it just high enough for Talise to reach.

"Thank you," she said.

The narwhal let out a soft, bleating noise. Talise understood it was saying "thank you, too." Then it dove beneath the waves and swam in a long, slow arc around the boat.

Suvanna sighed. So did Talise.

"I always wished I was a marine creature," Talise confessed. "Instead of a land creature. So I could stay in the ocean forever and ever."

Suvanna was silent for a moment. "If that's what you want . . . I can help you."

"Really?"

"I didn't tell the whole truth about my vacation earlier. But I sense you and I are kindred spirits, and I trust you." The light-house keeper unclasped the chain around her neck and tipped the gold-and-silver ring into her palm. "Before I came to Topsea years and years ago, this ring allowed me to live in the ocean."

"Like a mermaid?" Talise waited for Suvanna to laugh at her joke.

But Suvanna didn't laugh. She only smiled.

Talise frowned. "Are you saying this ring is . . . magic?"

Suvanna handed the ring to Talise. "I'm saying, if you want to live in the ocean forever and ever—you can."

The ring felt warm and tingly in Talise's palm. She squeezed her hand closed around it and breathed in the salty air. She imagined slipping into the water like the narwhal, and swimming off to explore the ocean forever and ever. The deep sea. The *deep*-deep sea. The deep-deep-*deepest* sea of all.

The idea made her feel happy.

Talise squeezed the ring again. In Topsea, she had Clara and Ms. Grimalkin and Principal King. She had two Loving/ Concerned parents (even if they were occasionally a bit Mystified).

And that wasn't all she had.

Back on shore, six kid-shaped blobs and one watch-hog-shaped blob stood at the water's edge. They waved at Talise.

Now Talise felt more than happy. She felt *joyful.*

"Living in the ocean used to be my lifelong dream," she told Suvanna, handing the ring back. "But not anymore. I would miss my best friends too much."

Suvanna tilted her head. "They must be wonderful friends if they're worth staying on land for."

Talise beamed. "They really are." She handed the ring back to Suvanna. Then she reached into her pocket and pulled out her sea blob.

"What's that?" Suvanna asked.

"It's an inanimate sea blob made of foam," Talise explained. "When you're feeling stressed, squeezing it helps you feel better." She paused. "It's also a thank-you gift. You helped me realize the purpose of my boat."

Suvanna took the sea blob. "Are you sure you don't need it?"

"I can always get another one." Talise smiled. "Or I suppose I could use a rubber duck. They're very comforting. At least, they think they are."

Suvanna laughed.

* * *

Runa peered through Jules's binoculars. "She's coming back!" she exclaimed. "Talise is coming back!"

Davy looked surprised. "Of course she is."

"She promised she'd take Earl Grey on another voyage," Nia said. Earl Grey snuffled in agreement.

"You didn't think she'd live on her boat forever, did you?" Quincy asked.

Runa shook her head. "I was worried she'd become a mermaid or something. Even though I know that's silly."

Jules stuck her pencil behind her ear. "Maybe not *that* silly."

"Talise is already the closest thing to a mermaid," Runa said. "Even if she has flippers and an air tank and a regulator and a BCD instead of fins!"

"Can I try the binoculars?" Finn asked.

Runa handed them over.

Finn kicked off his shoes and waded into the ocean until the water came up to his knees. (Which wasn't very deep, since Finn was so small.) He squinted through the binoculars, scanning the horizon.

He could've sworn he'd spotted a second boat far, far out on the water. But now all he saw was ocean.

"See anything?" Runa asked.

"Not anymore," Finn replied. "But I'm glad the lighthouse keeper is back—Topsea is about to get some visitors."

"Really?" Jules said. "How do you know?"

Finn shrugged. "I have a hunch."